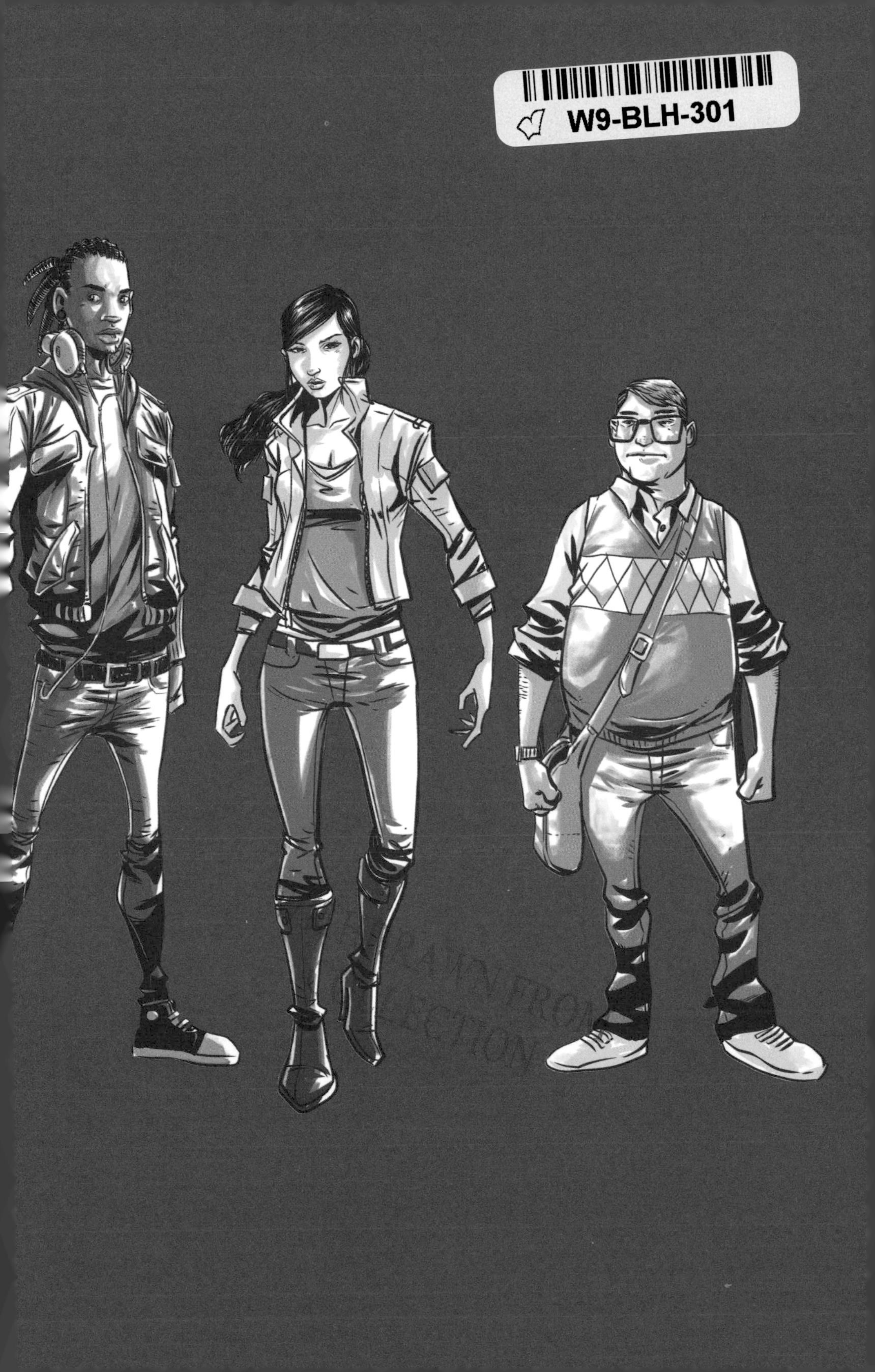

Disney

THE ZODIAC LEGACY

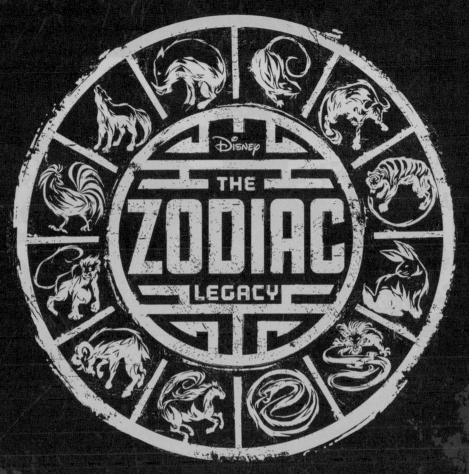

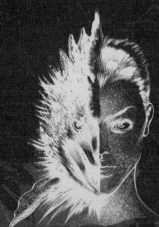

PAPERCUTZ

Disney Graphic Novels available from PAPERCUTZ

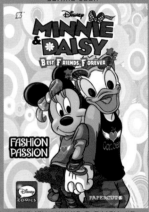

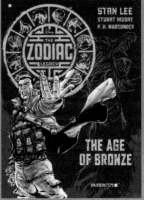

Disney

The Zodiac Legacy

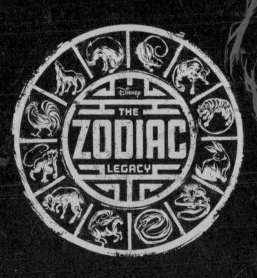

#2 "Power Lines"

Stan Lee — Creator

Stuart Moore — Writer

P.H. Marcondes — Artist

PAPERCUTZ™

New York

Disney
THE ZODIAC LEGACY

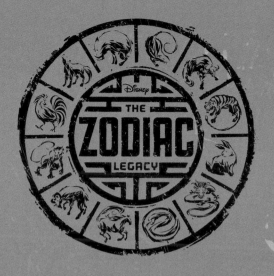

#2 "Power Lines"
Stan Lee – Creator
Stuart Moore – Writer
P.H. Marcondes – Artist
Andie Tong – Cover, Endpapers, and Character Profiles Artist
Jolyon Yates – Title Page Artist
Elaina Unger– Colorist
Bryan Senka – Letterer
Dawn Guzzo – Production
Melissa Kleynowski – Editorial Intern
Jeff Whitman – Editor
Jim Salicrup
Editor-in-Chief

ISBN: 978-162991-444-2 paperback edition
ISBN: 978-162991-445-9 hardcover edition

Papercutz books may be purchased for business or promotional use. For information on bulk purchases please contact Macmillan Corporate and Premium Sales Department at (800) 221-7945 x5442.

Printed in Korea through Four Colour Print Group
November 2016 by WE SP Co., Ltd

Distributed by Macmillan
First Printing

THE ZODIAC LEGACY

The power of the Zodiac comes from twelve pools of mystical energy. Due to a sabotaged experiment, twelve magical superpowers are unleashed on Steven Lee and twelve others.

TIGER

STEVEN

POWERS:

STRENGTH, REFLEXES

Now Steven Lee is thrown into the middle of an epic global chase. He'll have to master strange powers, outrun super-powered mercenaries, and unlock the secrets of the Zodiac Legacy. When Steven is first rescued by Jasmine and Carlos, he relishes his newfound powers and is excited to be on a grand adventure, alongside...

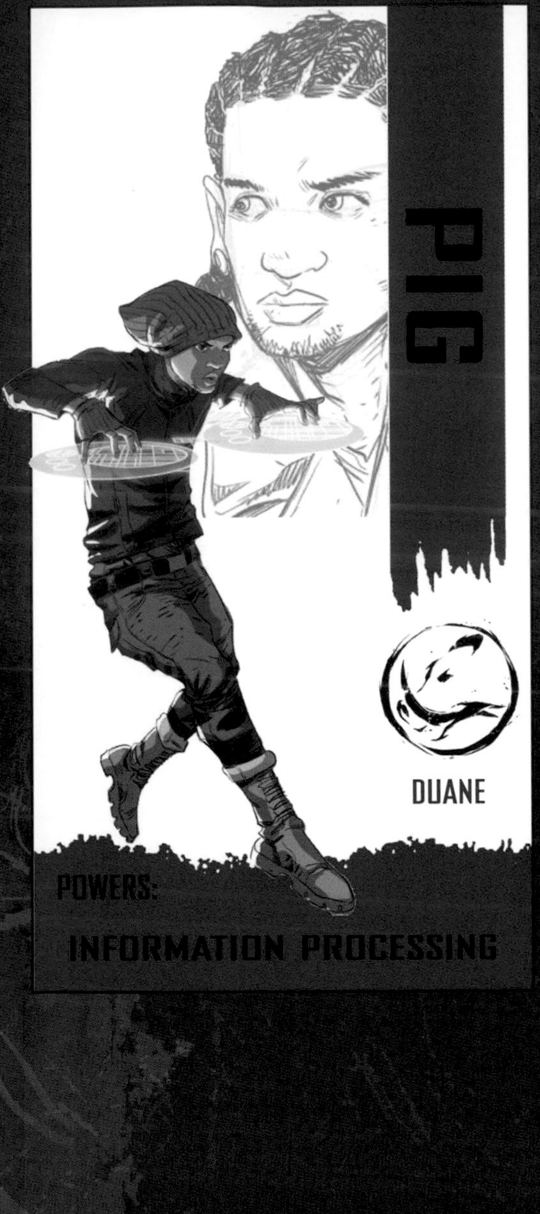
PIG
DUANE
POWERS:
INFORMATION PROCESSING

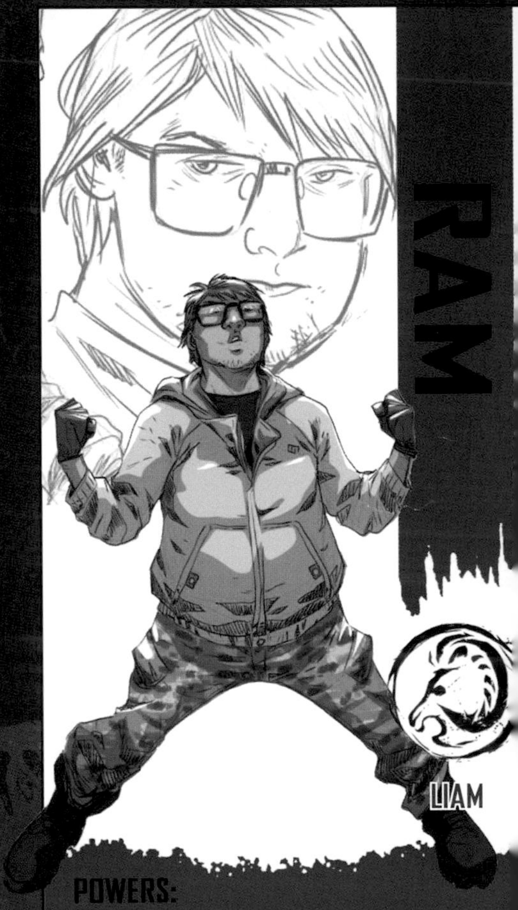
RAM
LIAM
POWERS:
INVULNERABILITY

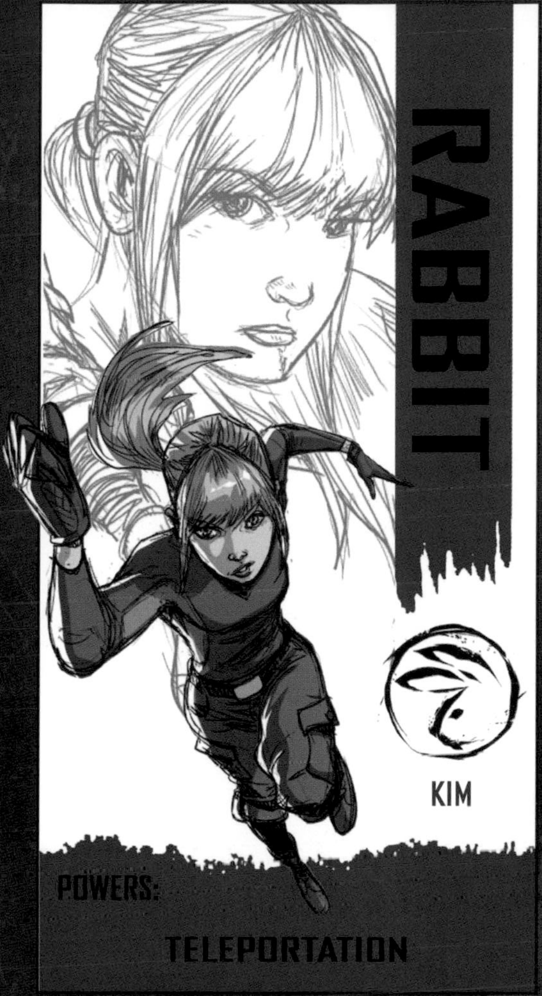
RABBIT
KIM
POWERS:
TELEPORTATION
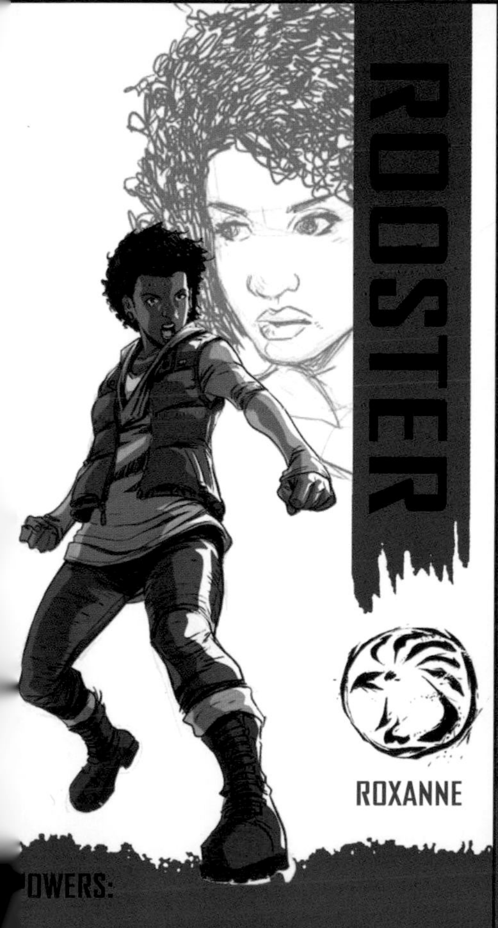
ROOSTER
ROXANNE
POWERS:
SONIC SCREAM

DRAGON

JASMINE

POWERS:
FIRE BREATHING, FLIGHT,
MIND CONTROL

The Vanguard organization is bent on tracking down all of the Zodiac powers. But one of its own has joined Steven Lee and friends...

OX

MALIK

POWERS: STRENGTH

Steven and his new friends will need to stay one step ahead of the Vanguard...

The Vanguard are...

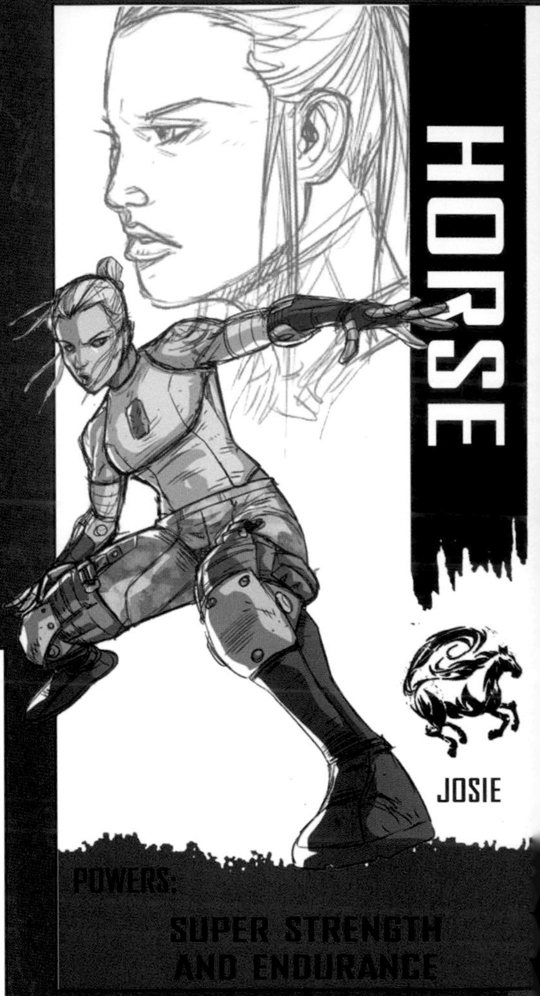
HORSE
JOSIE
POWERS:
SUPER STRENGTH AND ENDURANCE

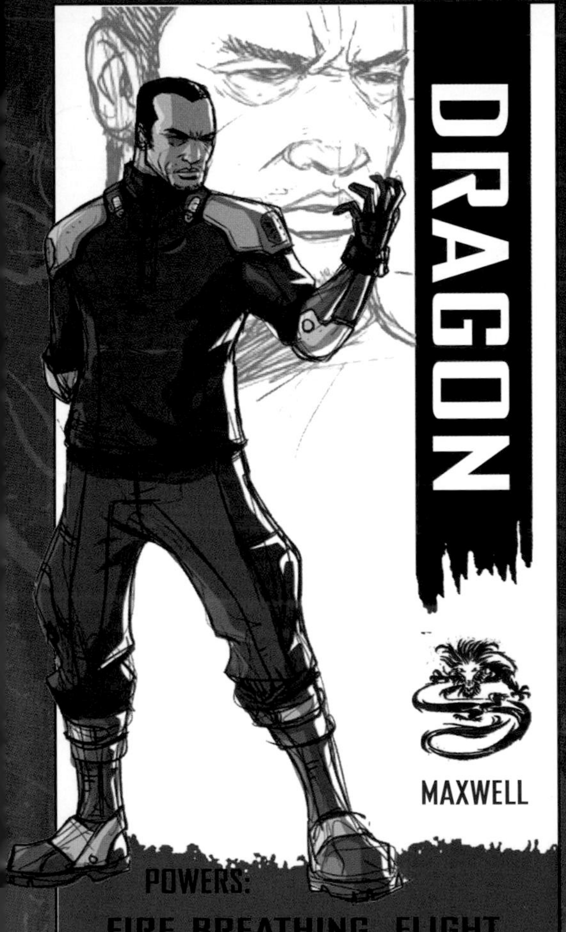
DRAGON
MAXWELL
POWERS:
FIRE BREATHING, FLIGHT, MIND CONTROL

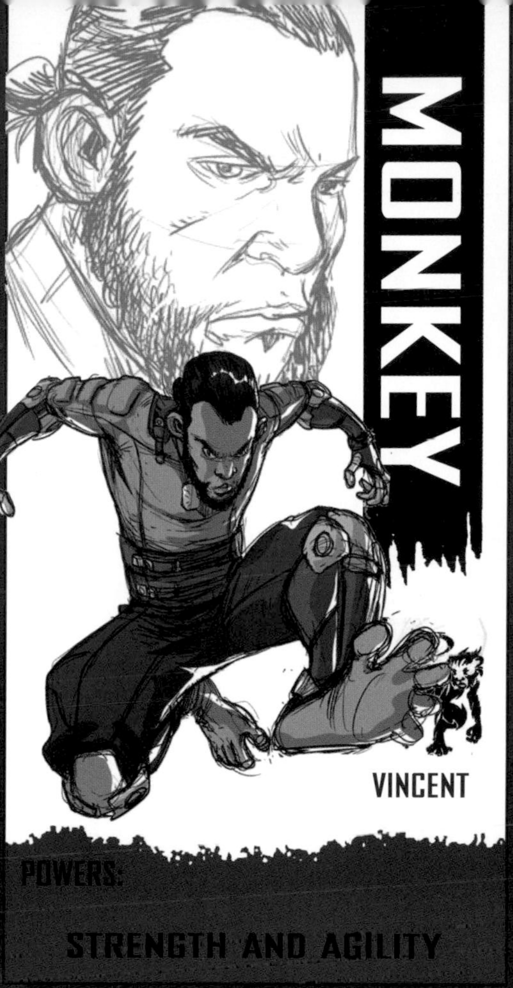
MONKEY
VINCENT
POWERS:
STRENGTH AND AGILITY

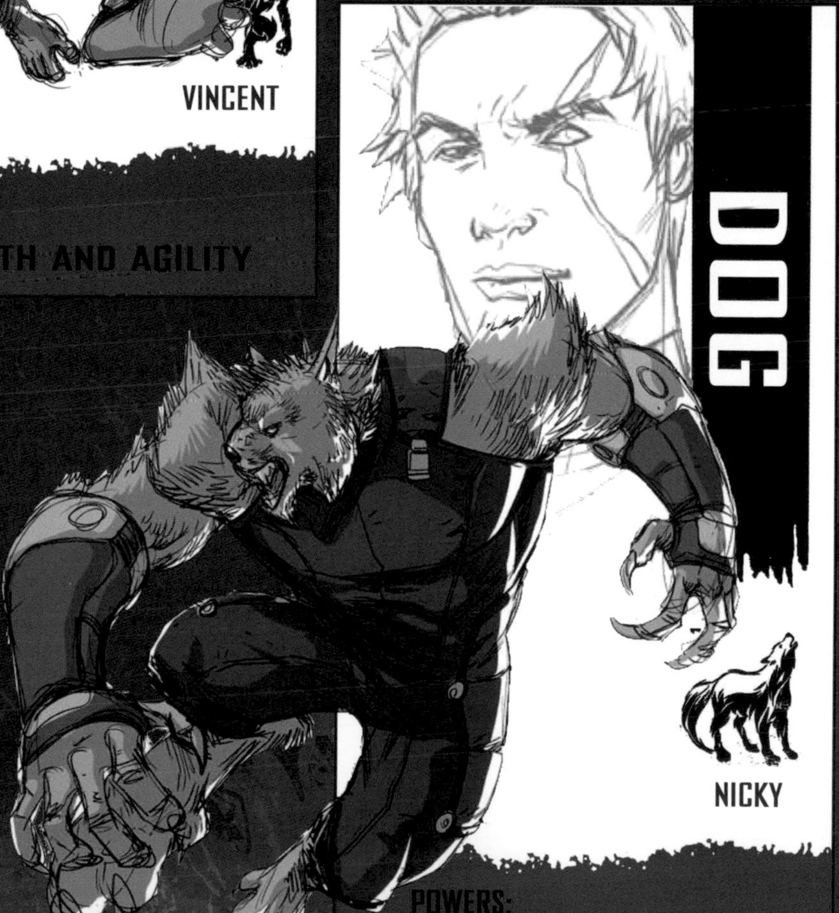
DOG
NICKY
POWERS:
ANIMAL TRANSFORMATION

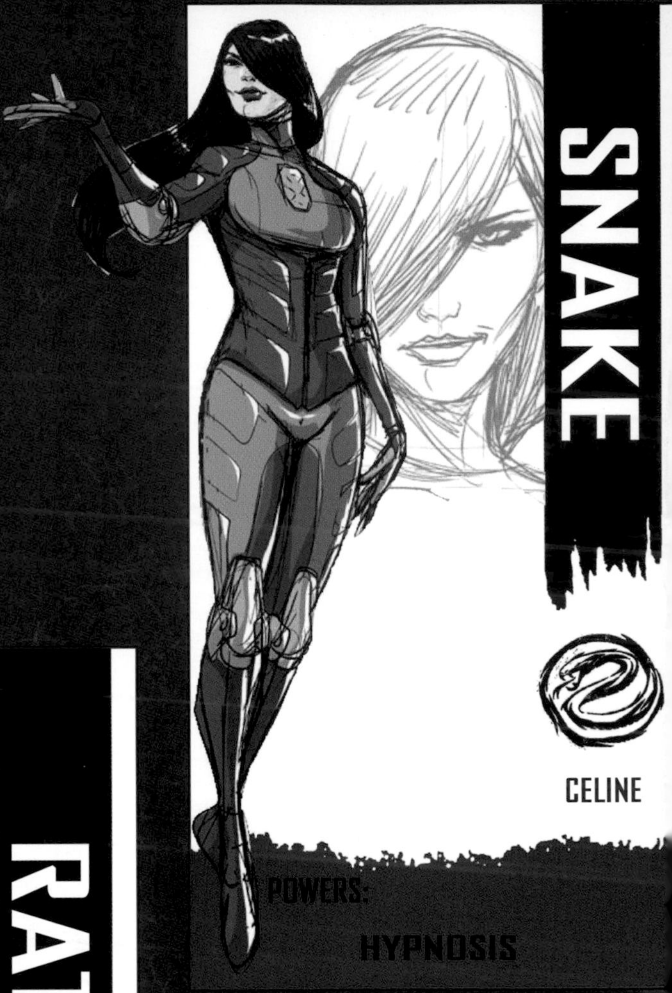
SNAKE
CELINE
POWERS:
HYPNOSIS

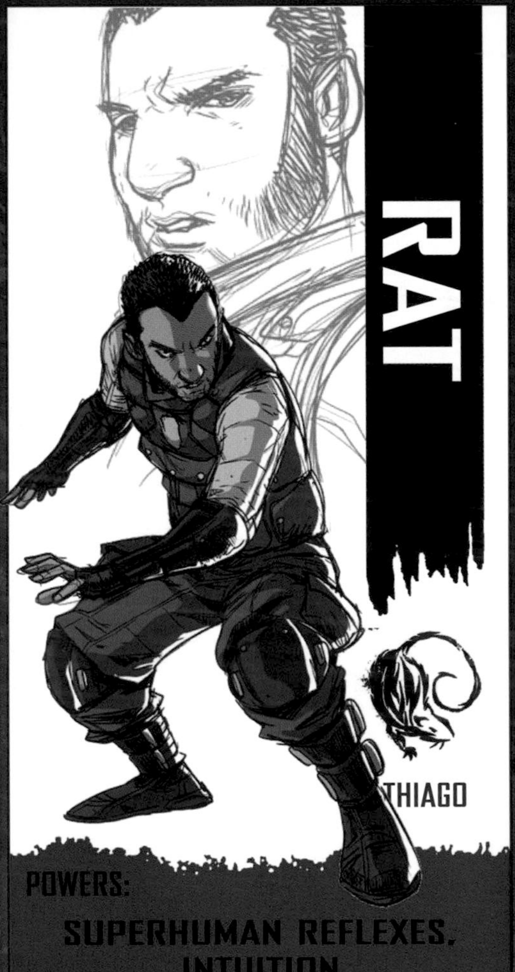
RAT
THIAGO
POWERS:
SUPERHUMAN REFLEXES,
INTUITION

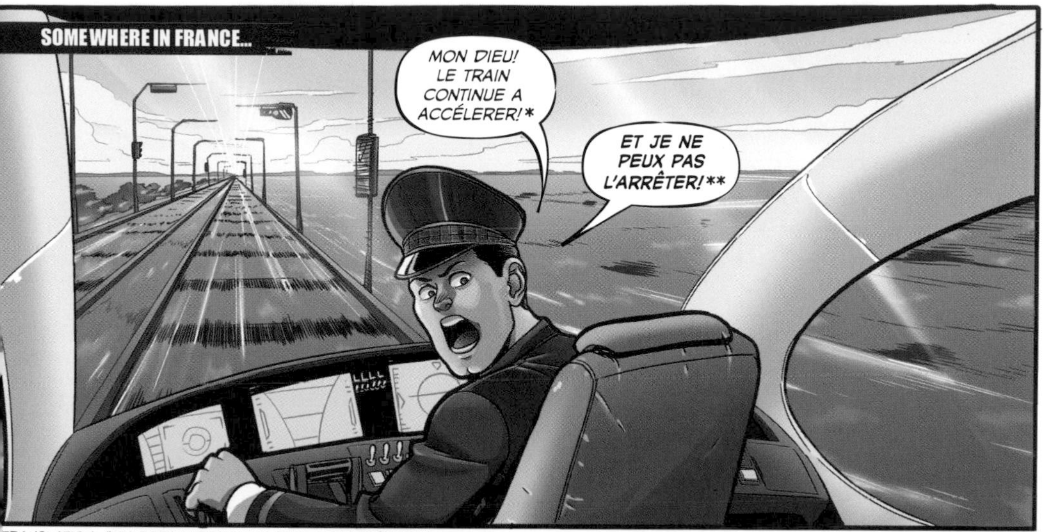
SOMEWHERE IN FRANCE...
MON DIEU! LE TRAIN CONTINUE A ACCÉLERER!*
ET JE NE PEUX PAS L'ARRÊTER!**

TRANSLATION: "MY GOD! THE TRAIN IS STILL ACCELERATING!" ** "AND I CAN'T STOP IT!"

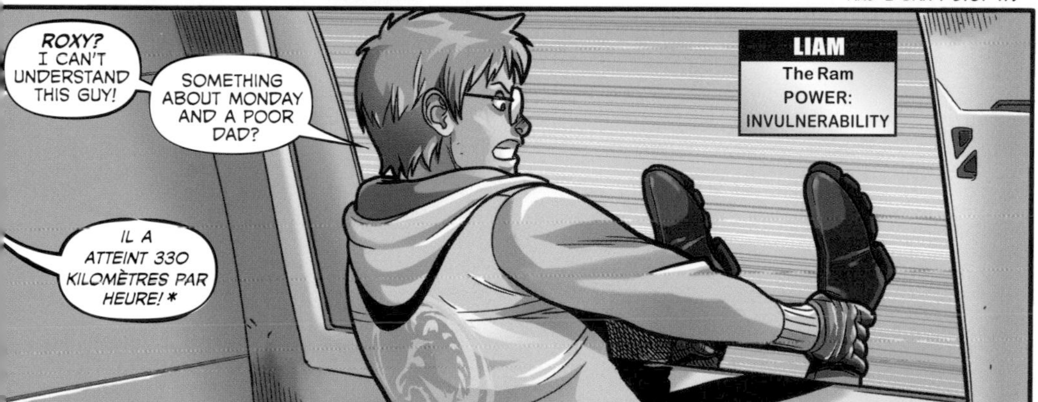
ROXY? I CAN'T UNDERSTAND THIS GUY!
SOMETHING ABOUT MONDAY AND A POOR DAD?
LIAM
The Ram
POWER:
INVULNERABILITY
IL A ATTEINT 330 KILOMÈTRES PAR HEURE! *

T'S UP TO OVER 205 MILES PER HOUR!"

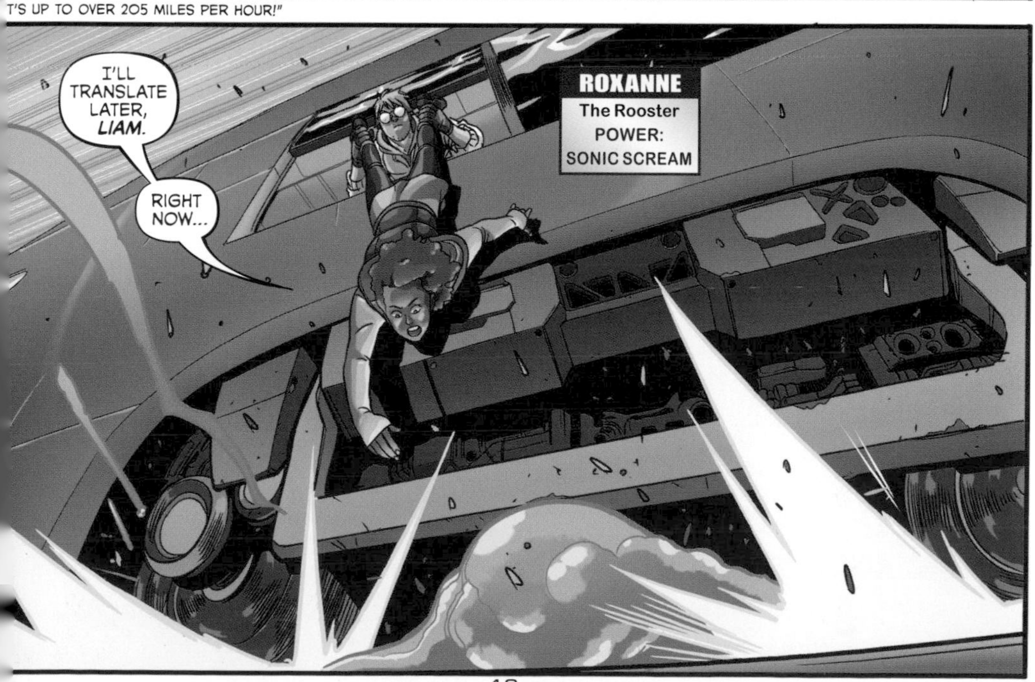
I'LL TRANSLATE LATER, LIAM.
RIGHT NOW...
ROXANNE
The Rooster
POWER:
SONIC SCREAM

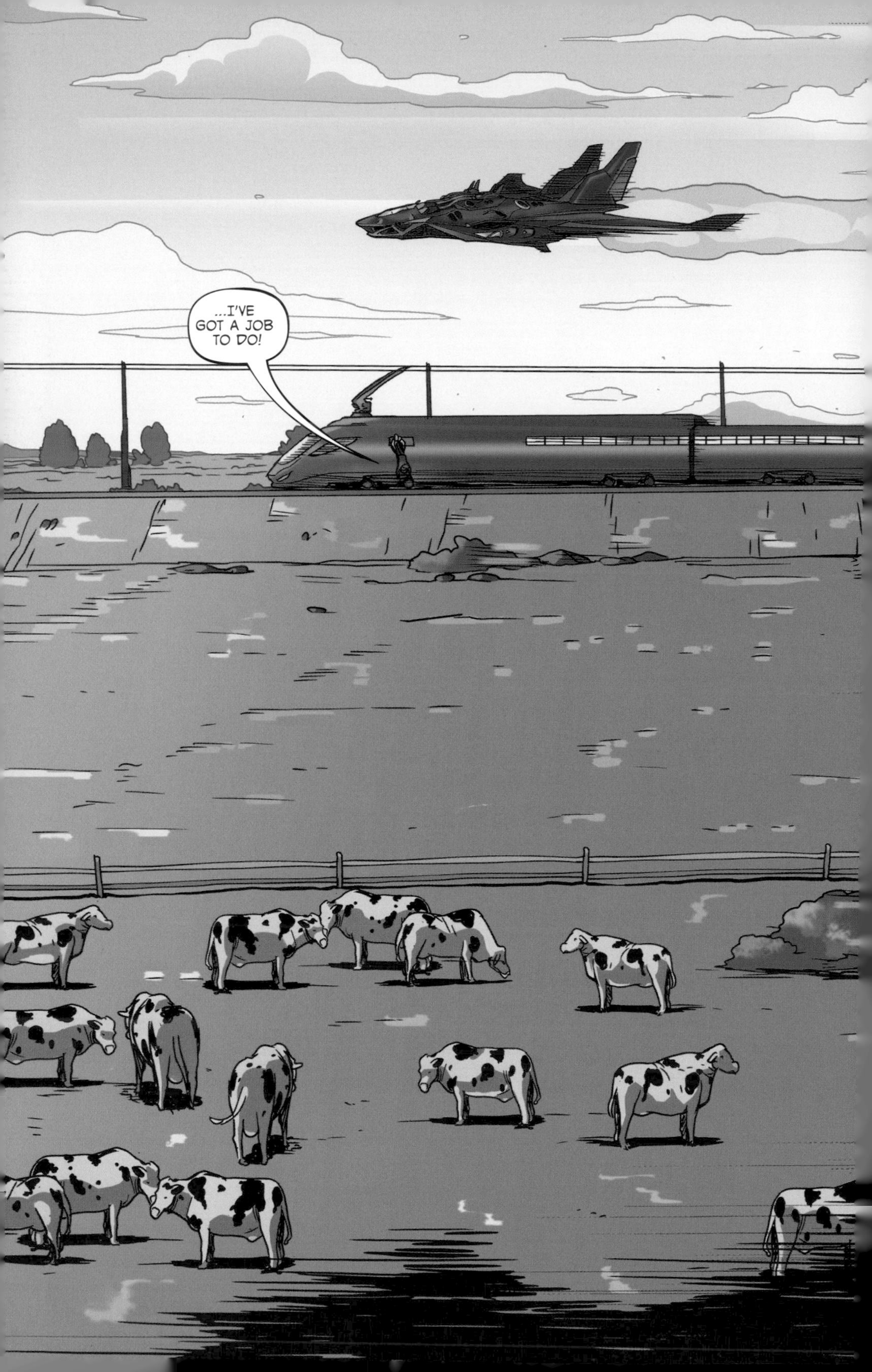
...I'VE GOT A JOB TO DO!

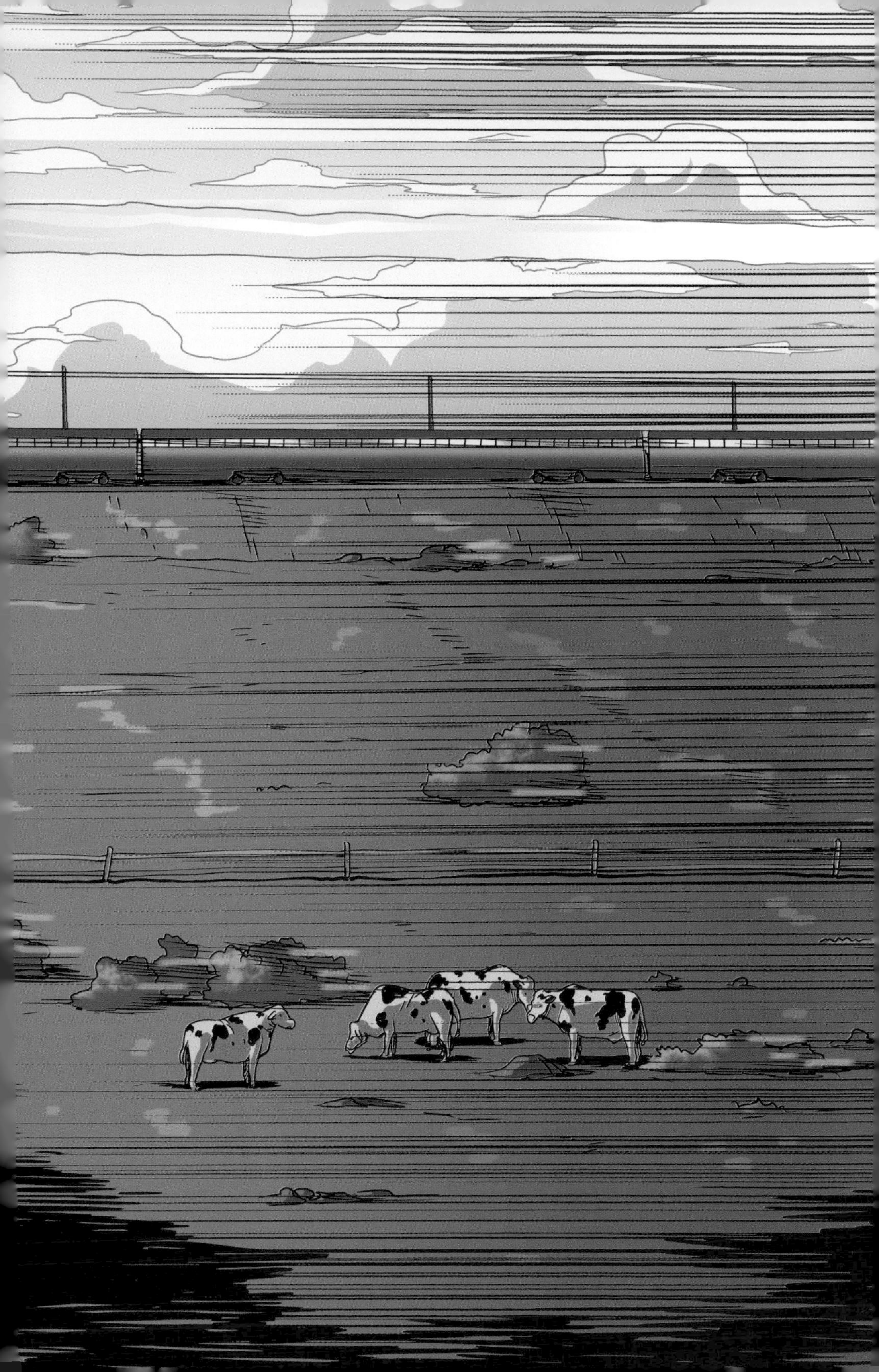

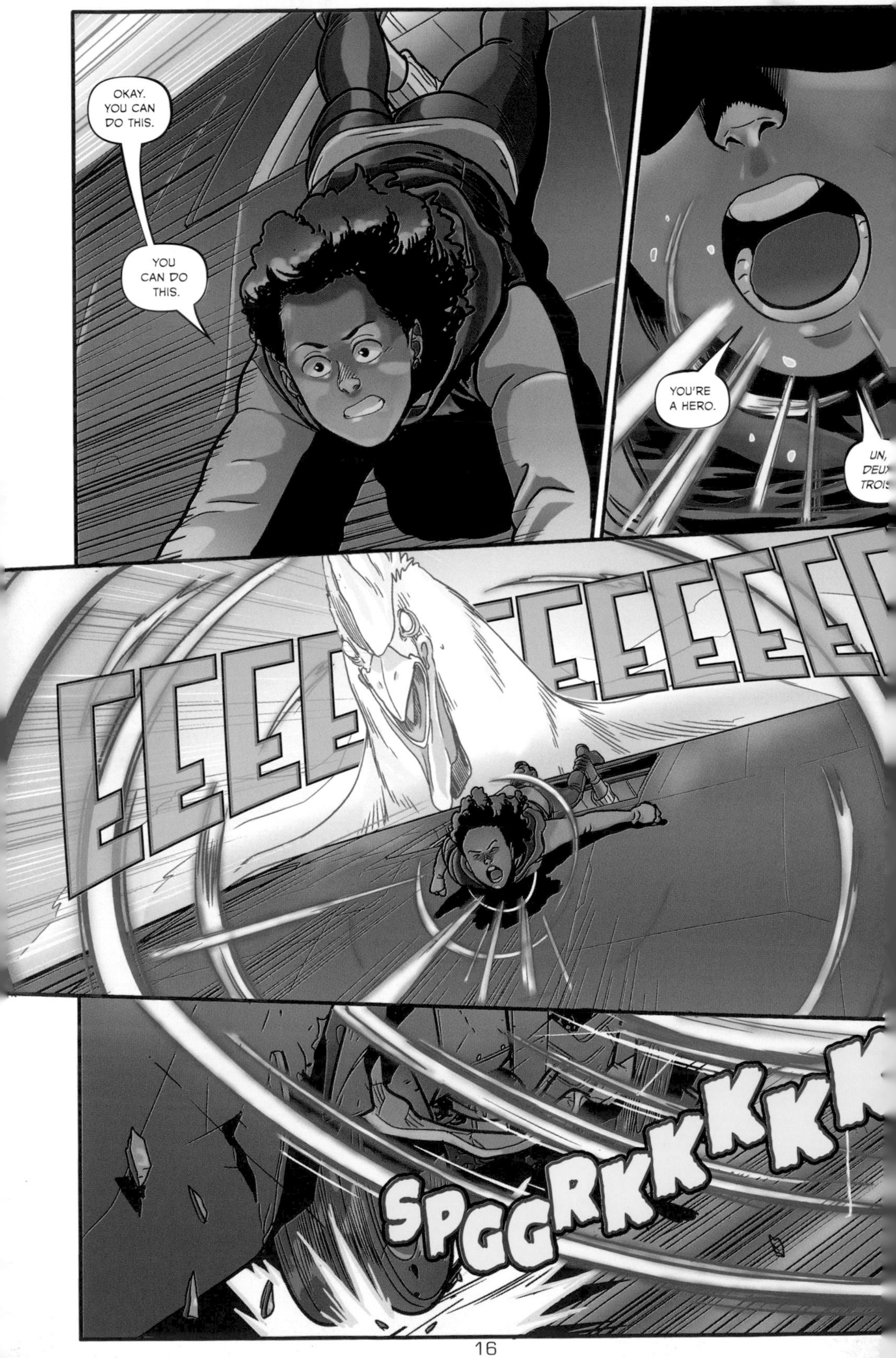
OKAY. YOU CAN DO THIS.
YOU CAN DO THIS.
YOU'RE A HERO.
UN, DEUX TROIS
EEEEEEEEEEE
SPGGRKKKKK

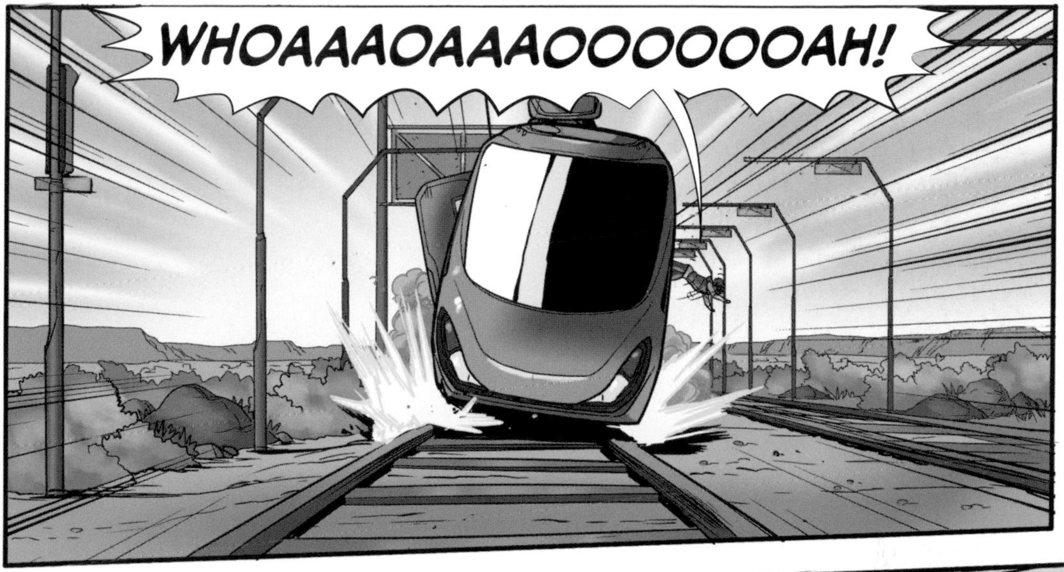
WHOAAAOAAAOOOOOOAH!

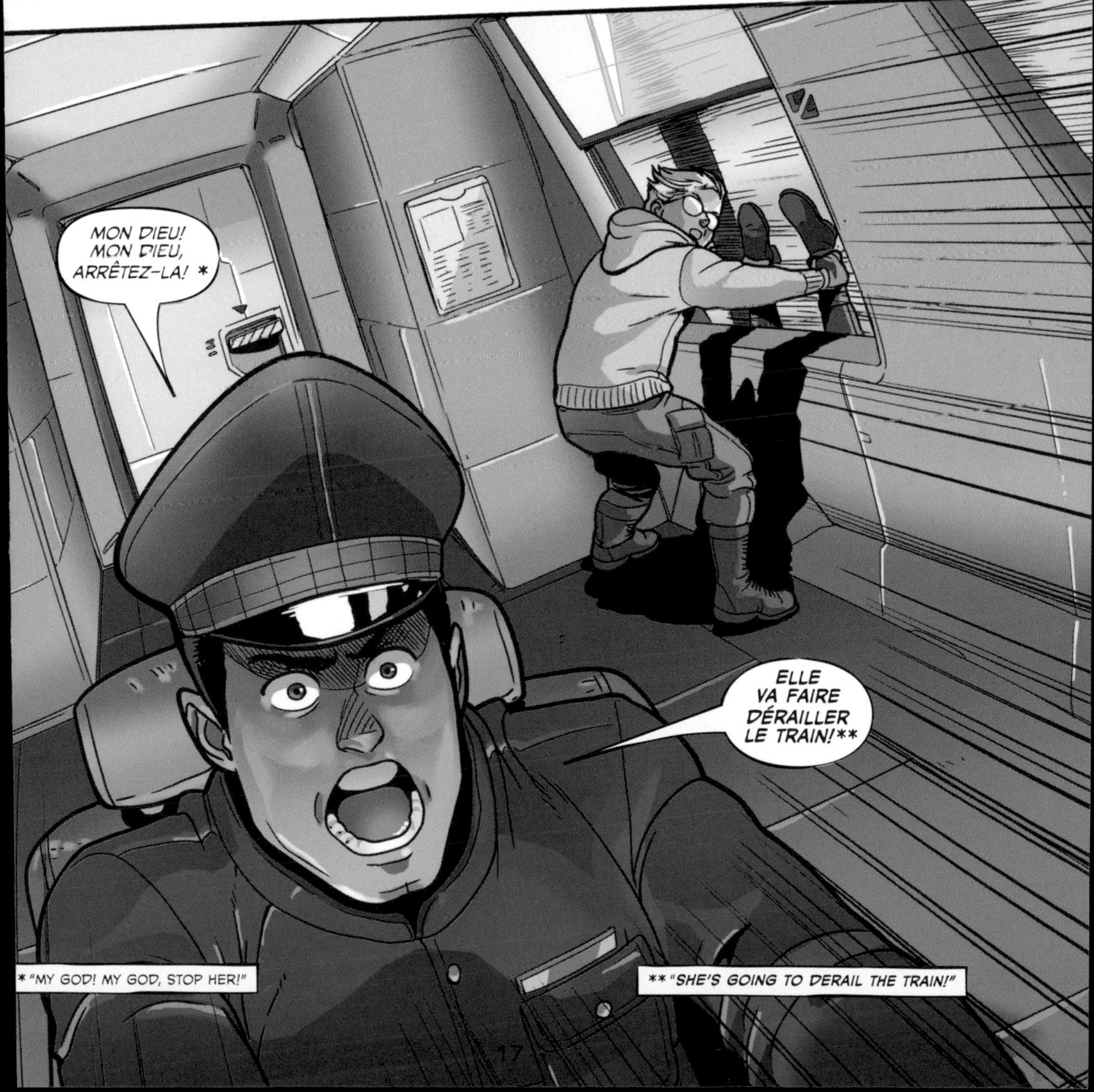
MON DIEU! MON DIEU, ARRÊTEZ-LA! *
ELLE VA FAIRE DÉRAILLER LE TRAIN!**
* "MY GOD! MY GOD, STOP HER!"
** "SHE'S GOING TO DERAIL THE TRAIN!"

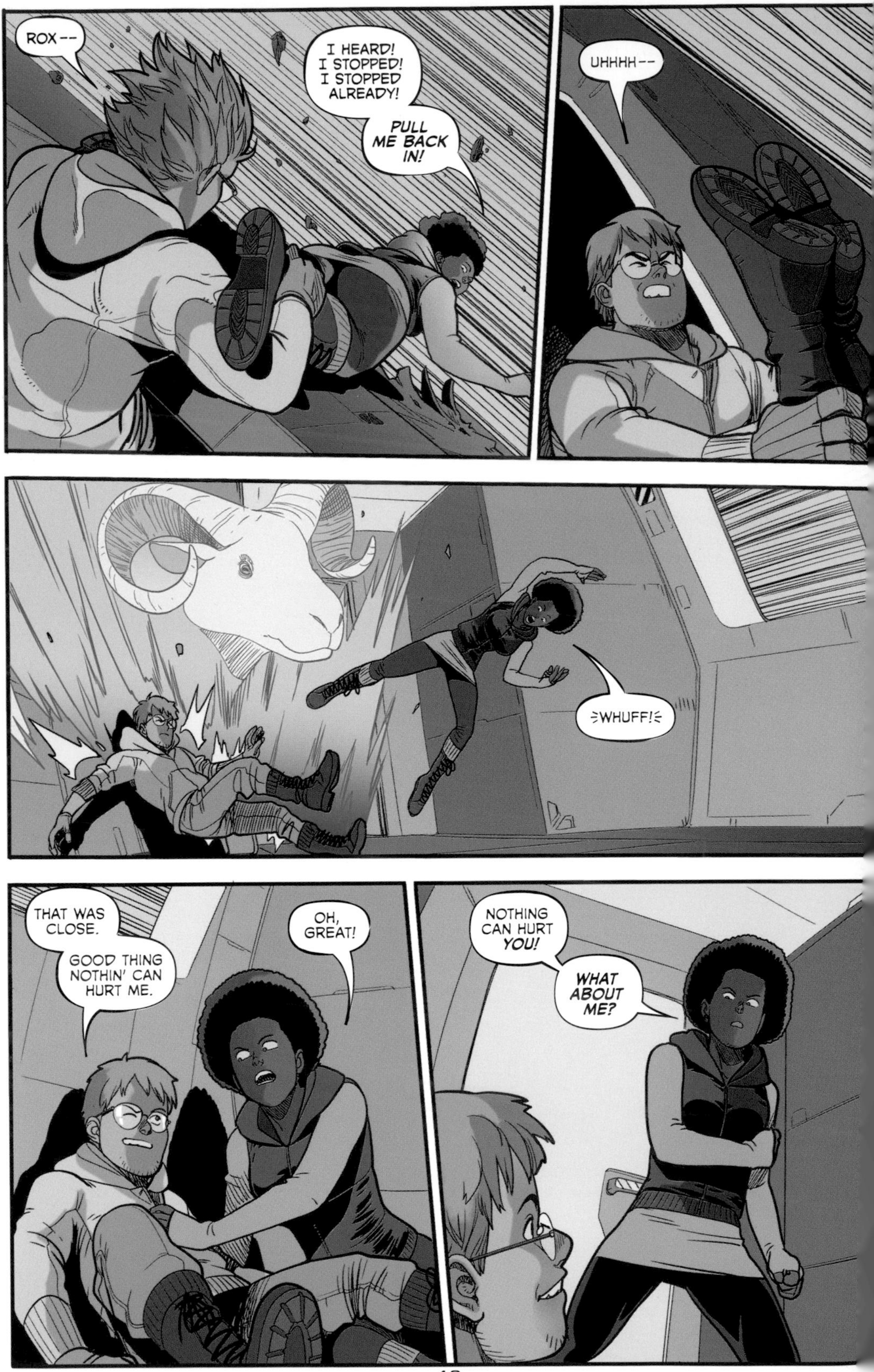
ROX--
I HEARD! I STOPPED! I STOPPED ALREADY!
PULL ME BACK IN!
UHHHH--
WHUFF!
THAT WAS CLOSE.
GOOD THING NOTHIN' CAN HURT ME.
OH, GREAT!
NOTHING CAN HURT YOU!
WHAT ABOUT ME?

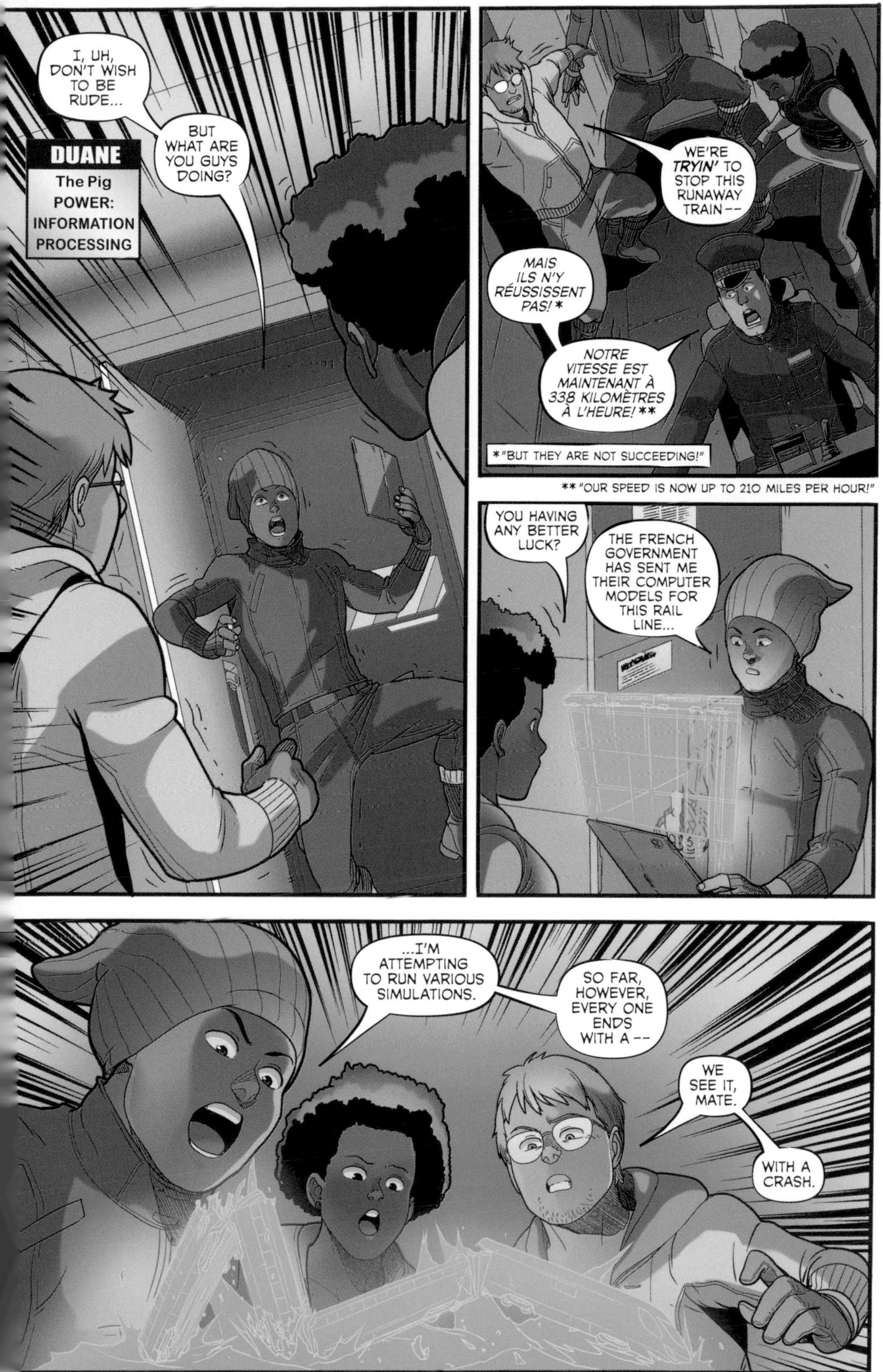
I, UH, DON'T WISH TO BE RUDE...
BUT WHAT ARE YOU GUYS DOING?
DUANE
The Pig
POWER: INFORMATION PROCESSING
WE'RE *TRYIN'* TO STOP THIS RUNAWAY TRAIN--
MAIS ILS N'Y RÉUSSISSENT PAS! *
NOTRE VITESSE EST MAINTENANT À 338 KILOMÈTRES À L'HEURE! **
*"BUT THEY ARE NOT SUCCEEDING!"
**"OUR SPEED IS NOW UP TO 210 MILES PER HOUR!"
YOU HAVING ANY BETTER LUCK?
THE FRENCH GOVERNMENT HAS SENT ME THEIR COMPUTER MODELS FOR THIS RAIL LINE...
...I'M ATTEMPTING TO RUN VARIOUS SIMULATIONS.
SO FAR, HOWEVER, EVERY ONE ENDS WITH A --
WE SEE IT, MATE.
WITH A CRASH.

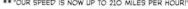

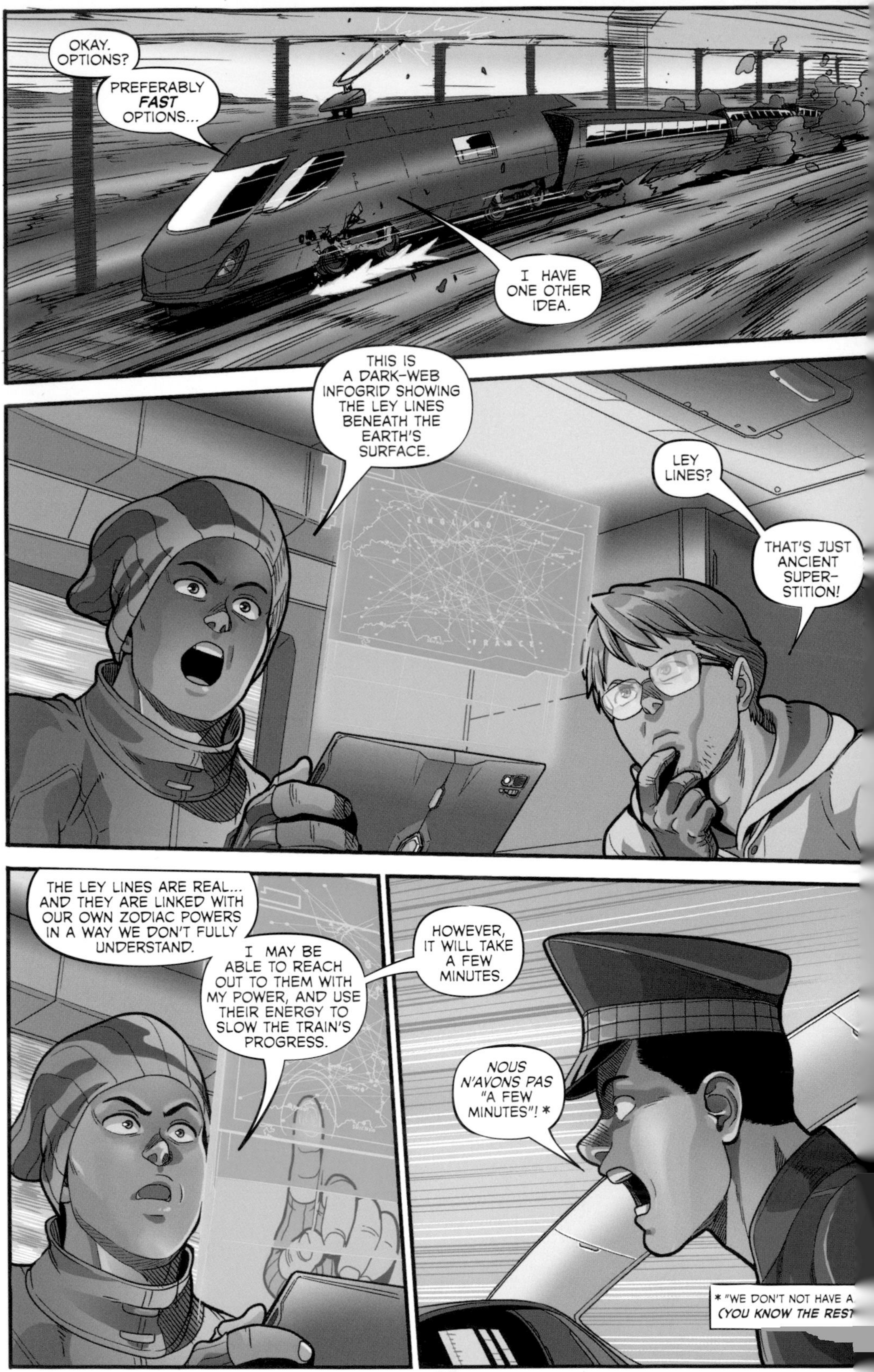
OKAY. OPTIONS?
PREFERABLY FAST OPTIONS...
I HAVE ONE OTHER IDEA.
THIS IS A DARK-WEB INFOGRID SHOWING THE LEY LINES BENEATH THE EARTH'S SURFACE.
LEY LINES?
THAT'S JUST ANCIENT SUPER-STITION!
THE LEY LINES ARE REAL... AND THEY ARE LINKED WITH OUR OWN ZODIAC POWERS IN A WAY WE DON'T FULLY UNDERSTAND.
I MAY BE ABLE TO REACH OUT TO THEM WITH MY POWER, AND USE THEIR ENERGY TO SLOW THE TRAIN'S PROGRESS.
HOWEVER, IT WILL TAKE A FEW MINUTES.
NOUS N'AVONS PAS "A FEW MINUTES"! *
* "WE DON'T NOT HAVE A
(YOU KNOW THE REST

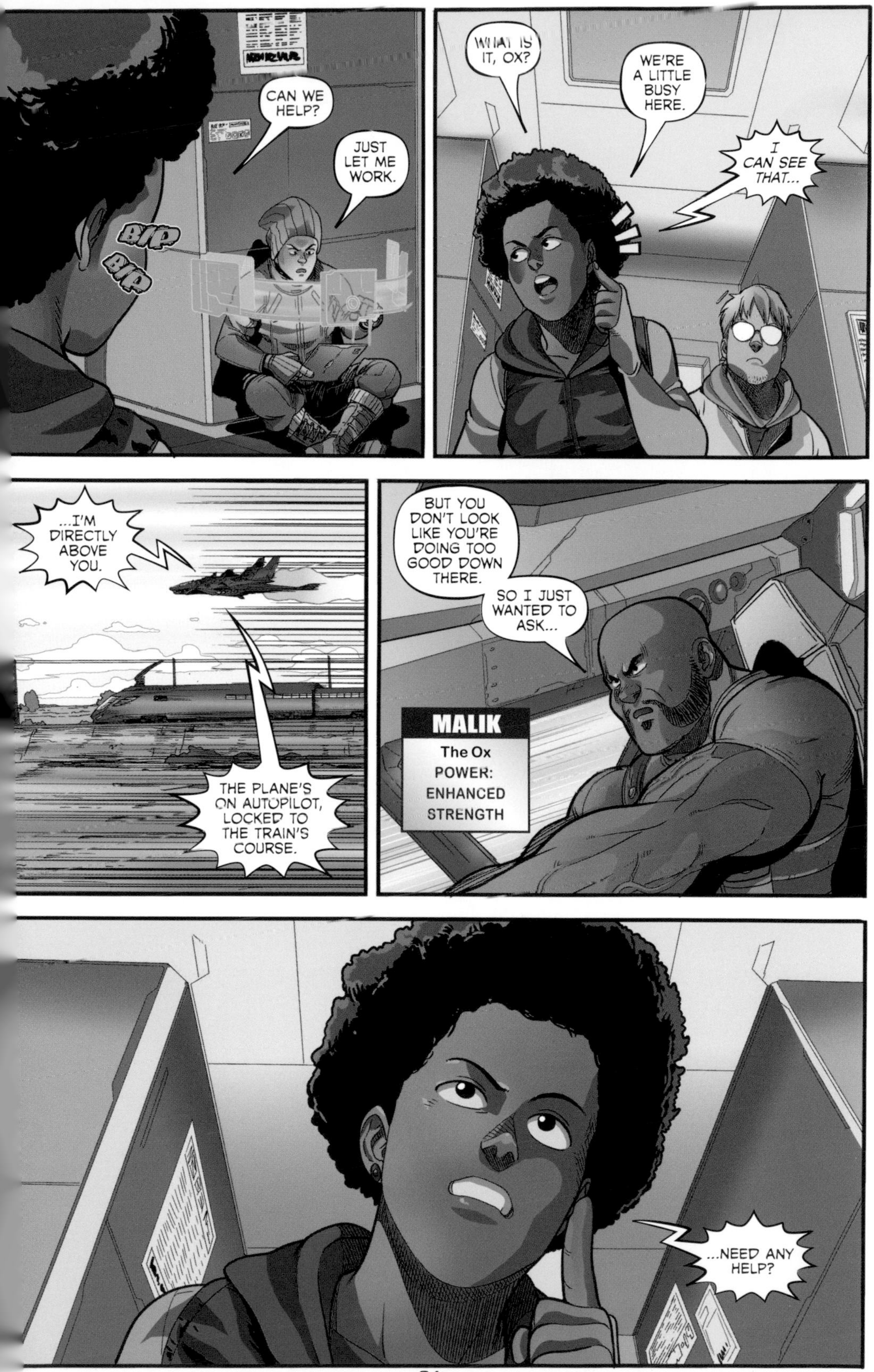
BIP
BIP
CAN WE HELP?
JUST LET ME WORK.
WHAT IS IT, OX?
WE'RE A LITTLE BUSY HERE.
I CAN SEE THAT...
...I'M DIRECTLY ABOVE YOU.
THE PLANE'S ON AUTOPILOT, LOCKED TO THE TRAIN'S COURSE.
BUT YOU DON'T LOOK LIKE YOU'RE DOING TOO GOOD DOWN THERE.
SO I JUST WANTED TO ASK...
MALIK
The Ox
POWER: ENHANCED STRENGTH
...NEED ANY HELP?

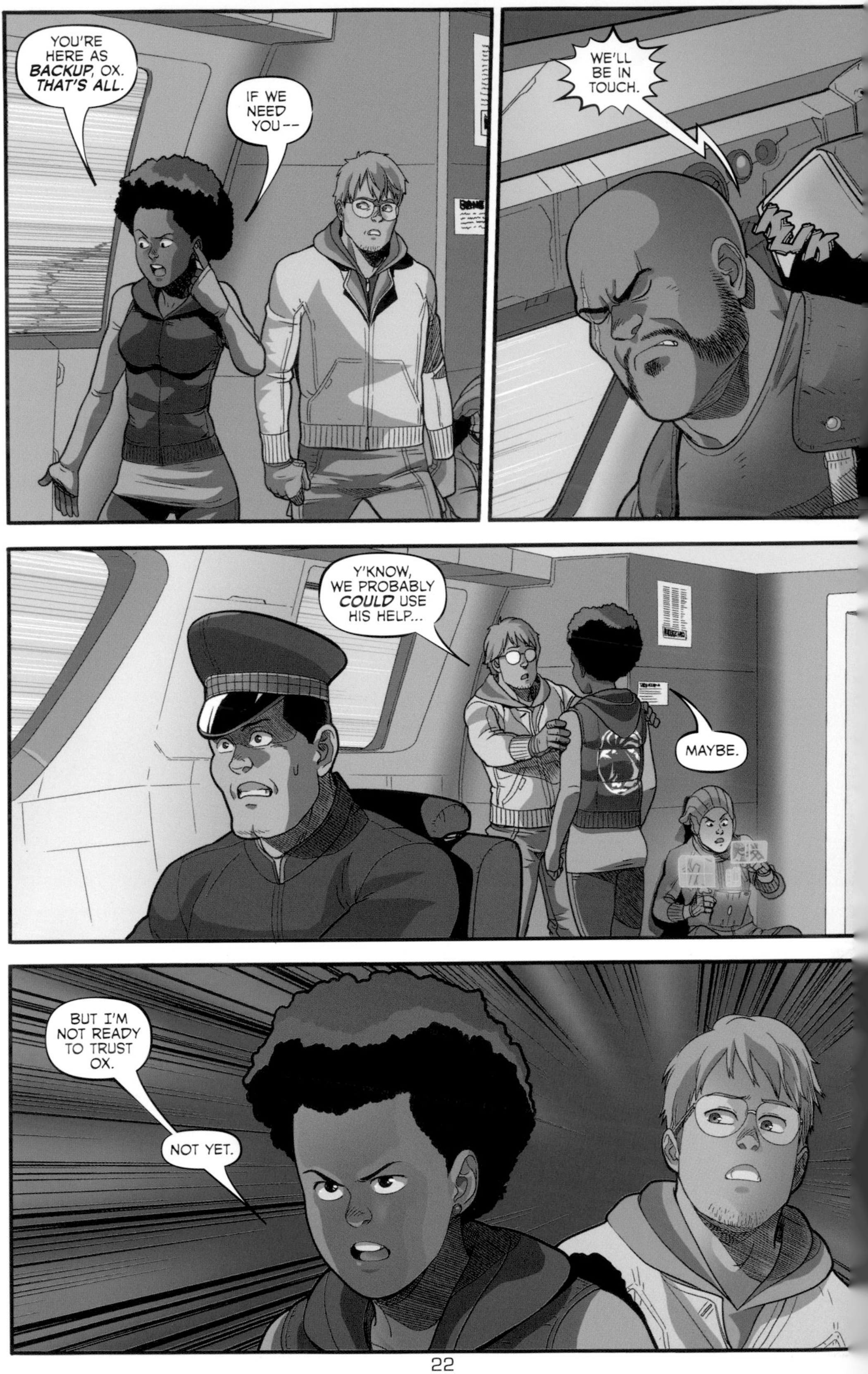

YOU'RE HERE AS **BACKUP**, OX. **THAT'S ALL**.
IF WE NEED YOU--
WE'LL BE IN TOUCH.
Y'KNOW, WE PROBABLY **COULD** USE HIS HELP...
MAYBE.
BUT I'M NOT READY TO TRUST OX.
NOT YET.

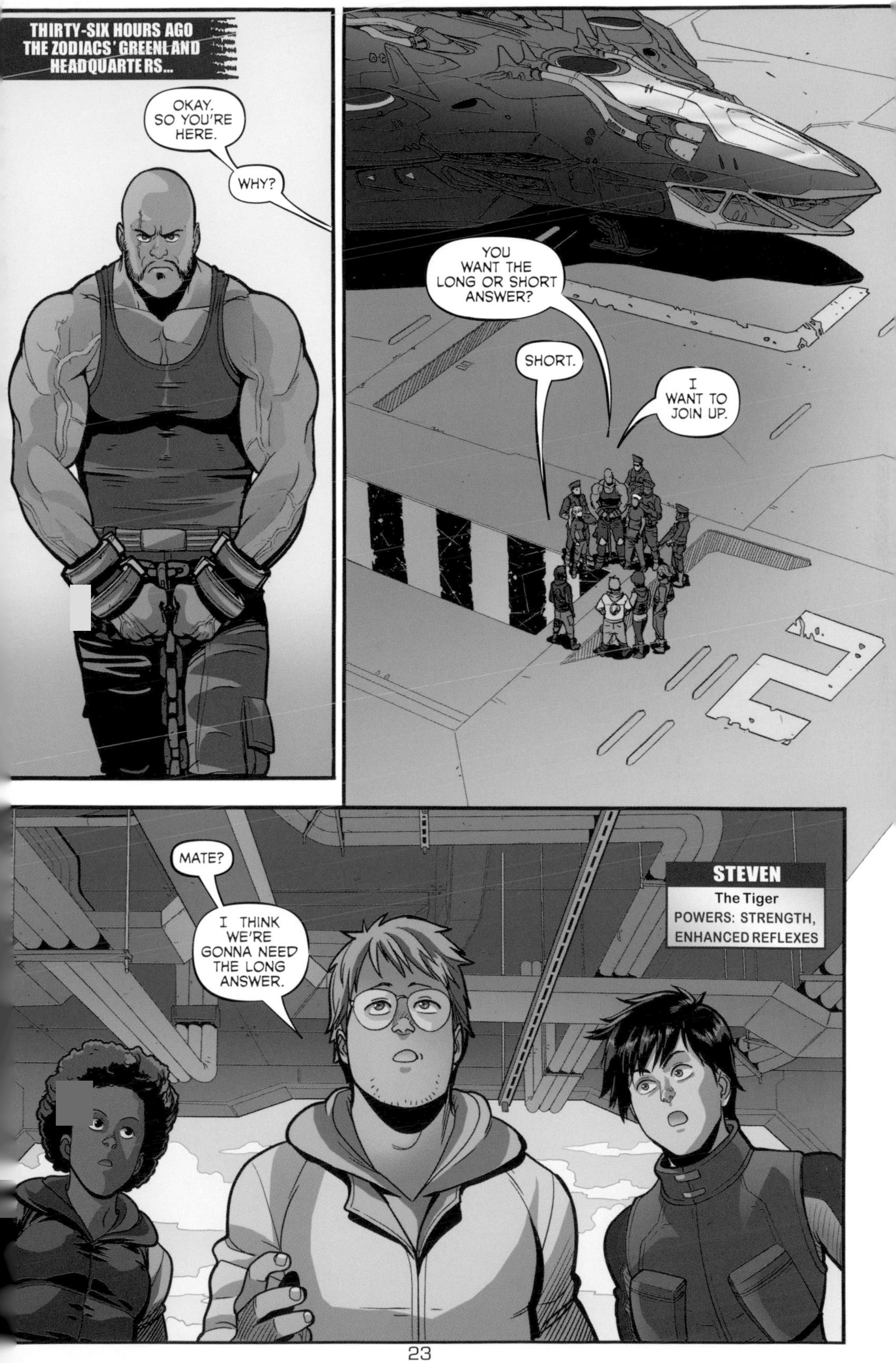
THIRTY-SIX HOURS AGO THE ZODIACS' GREENLAND HEADQUARTERS...
OKAY. SO YOU'RE HERE.
WHY?
YOU WANT THE LONG OR SHORT ANSWER?
SHORT.
I WANT TO JOIN UP.
MATE?
I THINK WE'RE GONNA NEED THE LONG ANSWER.
STEVEN
The Tiger
POWERS: STRENGTH, ENHANCED REFLEXES

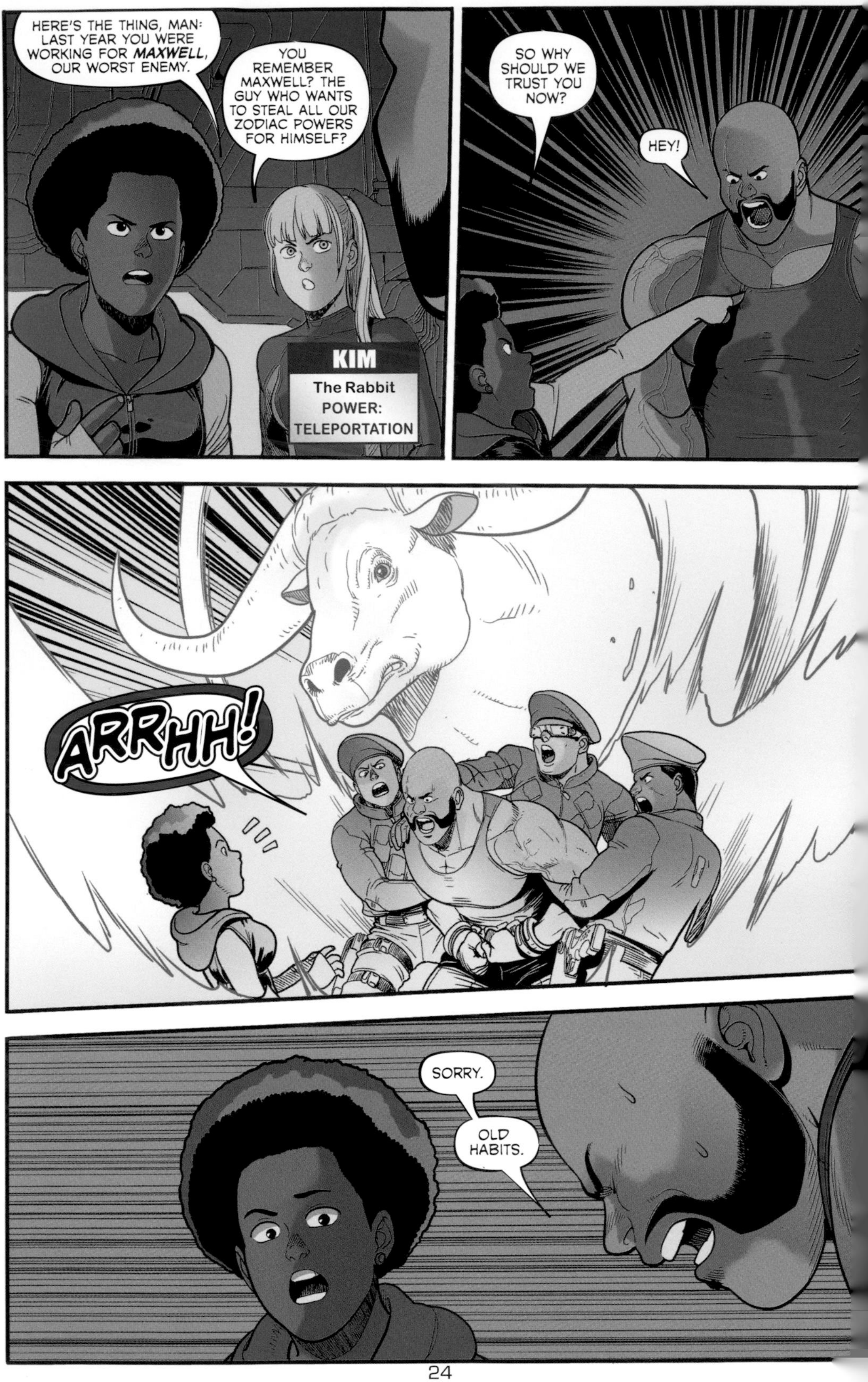
HERE'S THE THING, MAN: LAST YEAR YOU WERE WORKING FOR *MAXWELL*, OUR WORST ENEMY.
YOU REMEMBER MAXWELL? THE GUY WHO WANTS TO STEAL ALL OUR ZODIAC POWERS FOR HIMSELF?
KIM
The Rabbit
POWER: TELEPORTATION
SO WHY SHOULD WE TRUST YOU NOW?
HEY!
ARRHH!
SORRY.
OLD HABITS.

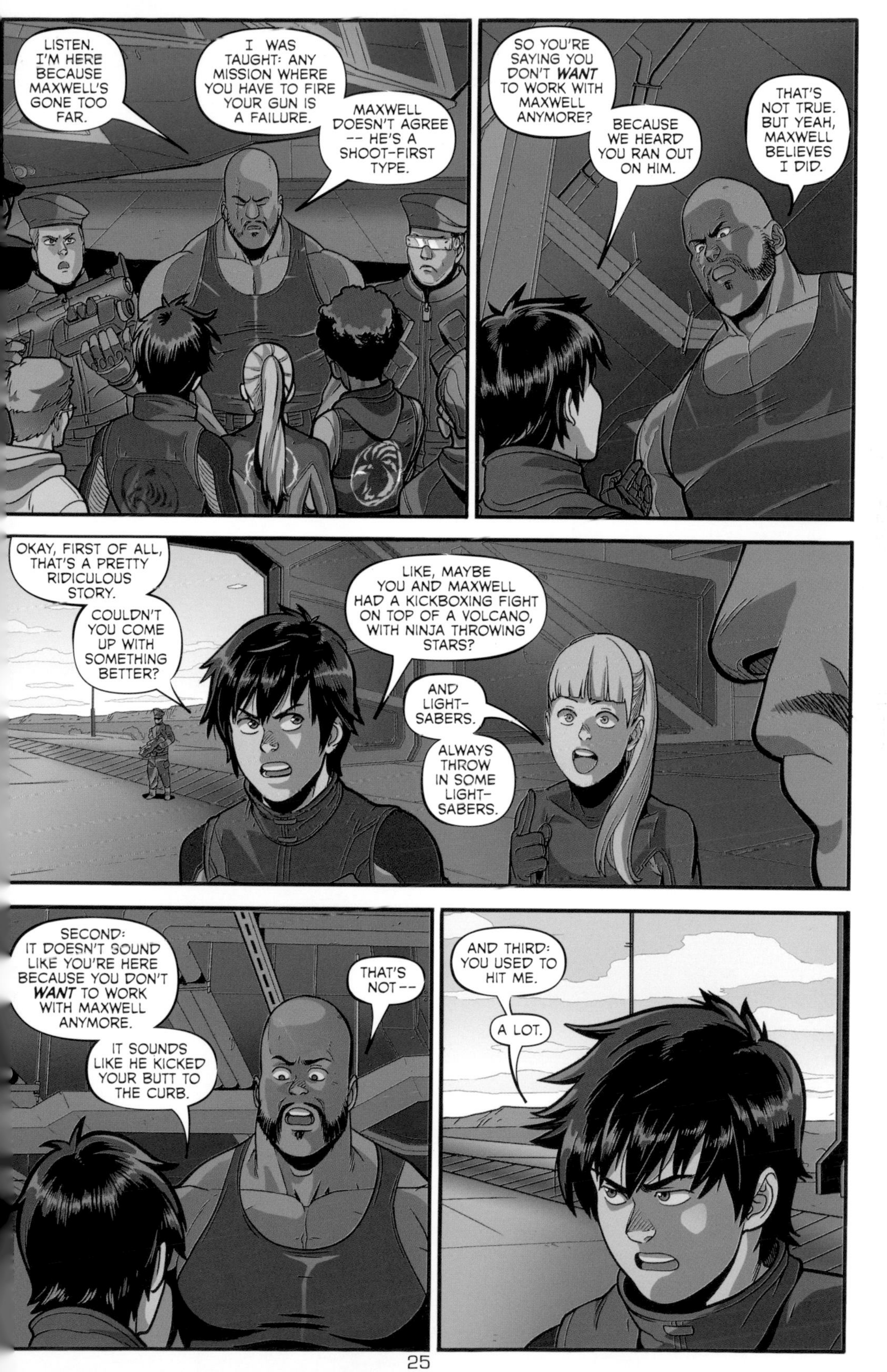
LISTEN. I'M HERE BECAUSE MAXWELL'S GONE TOO FAR.
I WAS TAUGHT: ANY MISSION WHERE YOU HAVE TO FIRE YOUR GUN IS A FAILURE.
MAXWELL DOESN'T AGREE -- HE'S A SHOOT-FIRST TYPE.
SO YOU'RE SAYING YOU DON'T **WANT** TO WORK WITH MAXWELL ANYMORE?
BECAUSE WE HEARD YOU RAN OUT ON HIM.
THAT'S NOT TRUE. BUT YEAH, MAXWELL BELIEVES I DID.
OKAY, FIRST OF ALL, THAT'S A PRETTY RIDICULOUS STORY.
COULDN'T YOU COME UP WITH SOMETHING BETTER?
LIKE, MAYBE YOU AND MAXWELL HAD A KICKBOXING FIGHT ON TOP OF A VOLCANO, WITH NINJA THROWING STARS?
AND LIGHT-SABERS.
ALWAYS THROW IN SOME LIGHT-SABERS.
SECOND: IT DOESN'T SOUND LIKE YOU'RE HERE BECAUSE YOU DON'T **WANT** TO WORK WITH MAXWELL ANYMORE.
IT SOUNDS LIKE HE KICKED YOUR BUTT TO THE CURB.
THAT'S NOT--
AND THIRD: YOU USED TO HIT ME.
A LOT.

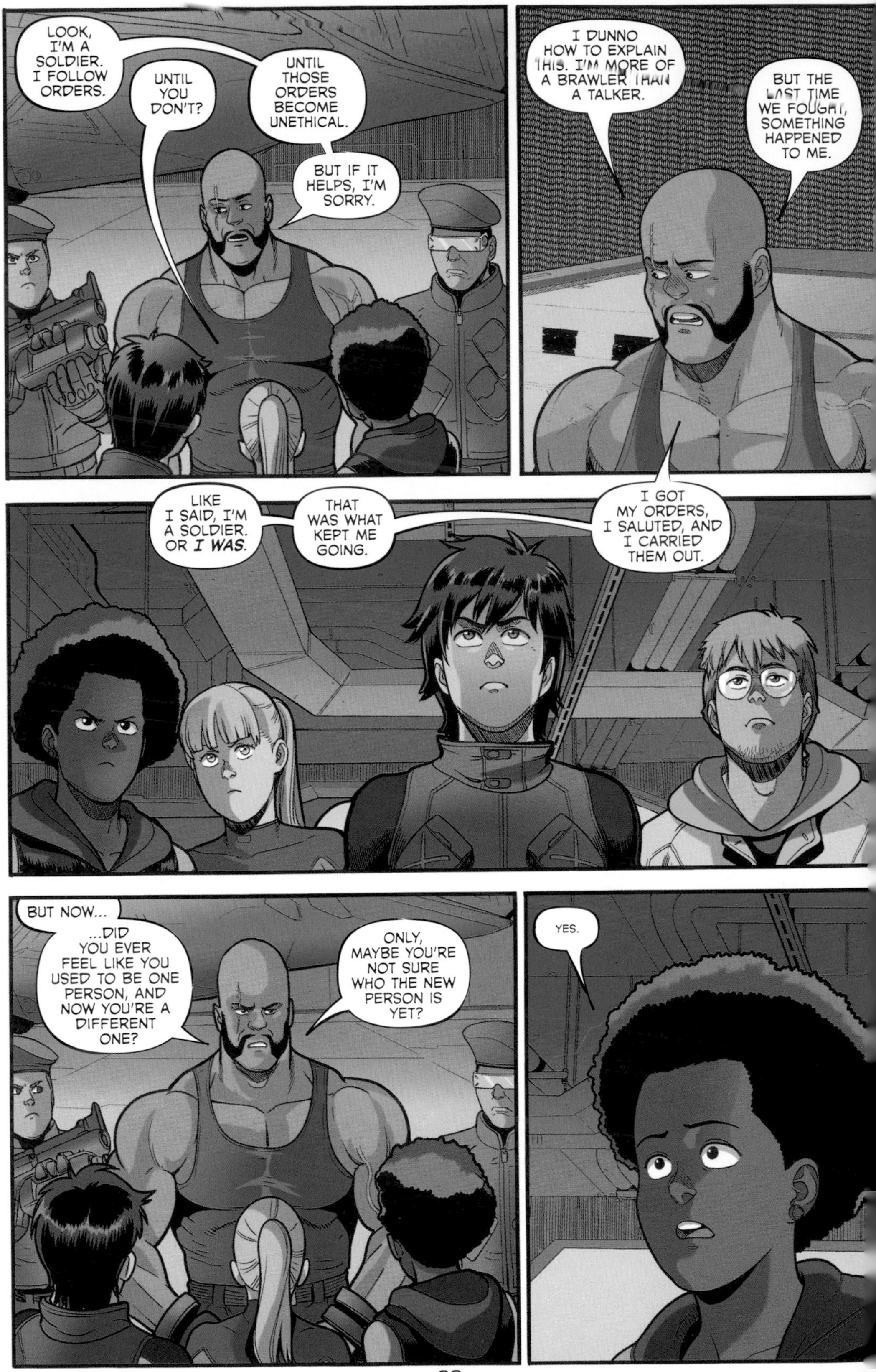
LOOK, I'M A SOLDIER. I FOLLOW ORDERS.
UNTIL YOU DON'T?
UNTIL THOSE ORDERS BECOME UNETHICAL.
BUT IF IT HELPS, I'M SORRY.
I DUNNO HOW TO EXPLAIN THIS. I'M MORE OF A BRAWLER THAN A TALKER.
BUT THE LAST TIME WE FOUGHT, SOMETHING HAPPENED TO ME.
LIKE I SAID, I'M A SOLDIER. OR I WAS.
THAT WAS WHAT KEPT ME GOING.
I GOT MY ORDERS, I SALUTED, AND I CARRIED THEM OUT.
BUT NOW...
...DID YOU EVER FEEL LIKE YOU USED TO BE ONE PERSON, AND NOW YOU'RE A DIFFERENT ONE?
ONLY, MAYBE YOU'RE NOT SURE WHO THE NEW PERSON IS YET?
YES.

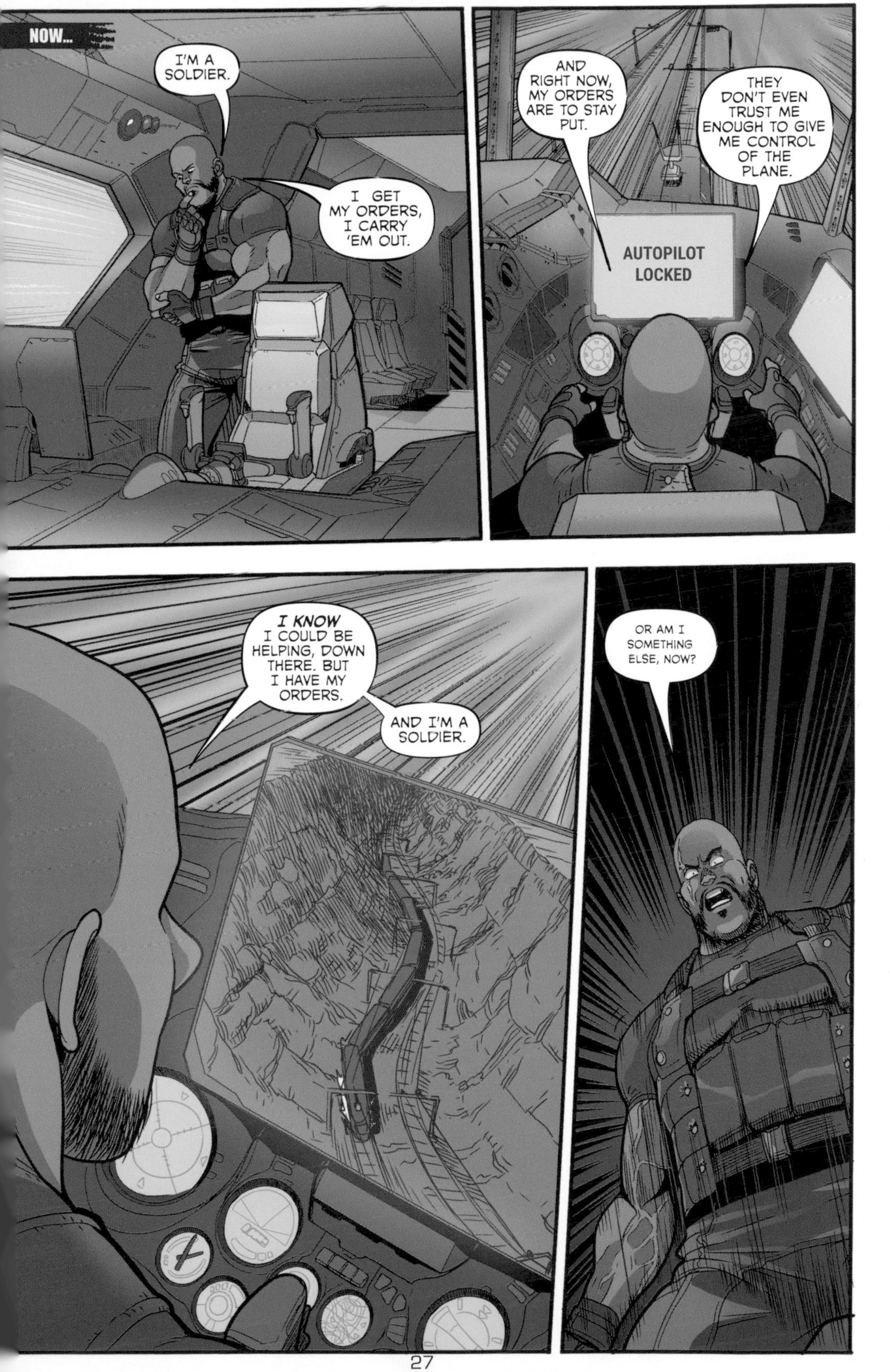

NOW...
I'M A SOLDIER.
I GET MY ORDERS, I CARRY 'EM OUT.
AND RIGHT NOW, MY ORDERS ARE TO STAY PUT.
THEY DON'T EVEN TRUST ME ENOUGH TO GIVE ME CONTROL OF THE PLANE.
AUTOPILOT LOCKED
I KNOW I COULD BE HELPING, DOWN THERE. BUT I HAVE MY ORDERS.
AND I'M A SOLDIER.
OR AM I SOMETHING ELSE, NOW?

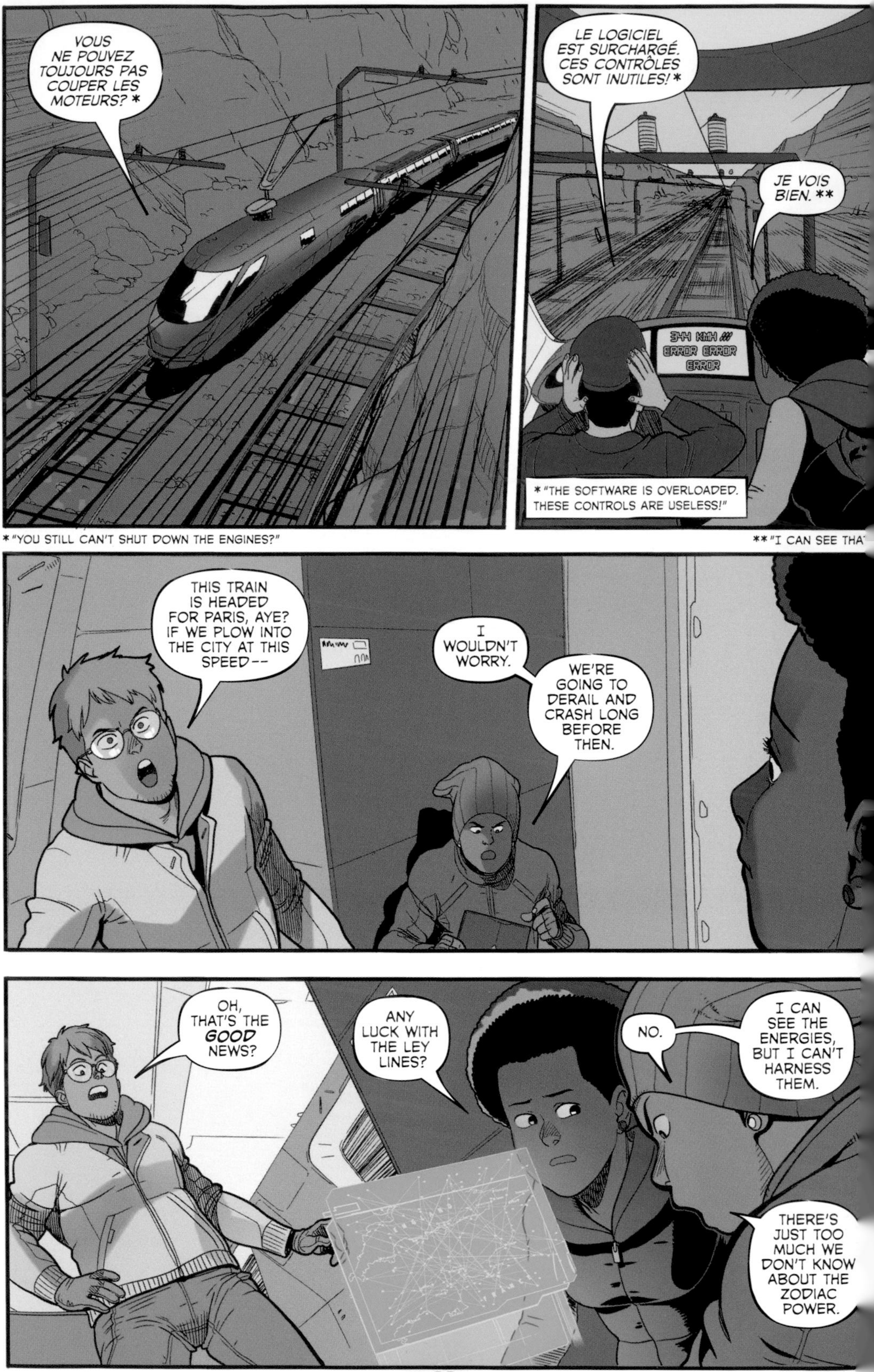
VOUS NE POUVEZ TOUJOURS PAS COUPER LES MOTEURS? *
LE LOGICIEL EST SURCHARGÉ. CES CONTRÔLES SONT INUTILES! *
JE VOIS BIEN. **
344 KMH
ERROR ERROR ERROR
* "THE SOFTWARE IS OVERLOADED. THESE CONTROLS ARE USELESS!"
* "YOU STILL CAN'T SHUT DOWN THE ENGINES?"
** "I CAN SEE THA
THIS TRAIN IS HEADED FOR PARIS, AYE? IF WE PLOW INTO THE CITY AT THIS SPEED--
I WOULDN'T WORRY.
WE'RE GOING TO DERAIL AND CRASH LONG BEFORE THEN.
OH, THAT'S THE *GOOD* NEWS?
ANY LUCK WITH THE LEY LINES?
NO.
I CAN SEE THE ENERGIES, BUT I CAN'T HARNESS THEM.
THERE'S JUST TOO MUCH WE DON'T KNOW ABOUT THE ZODIAC POWER.

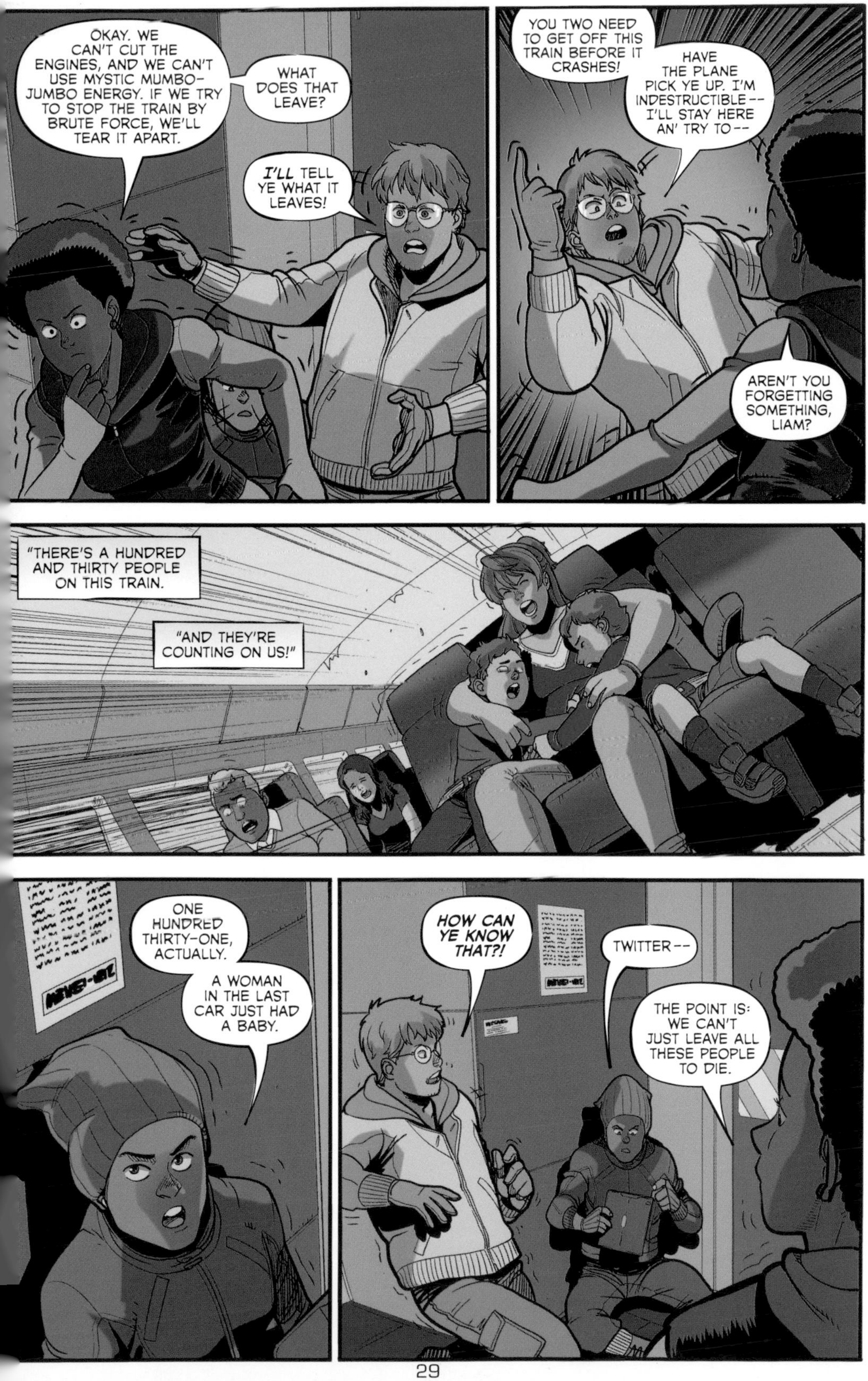
OKAY. WE CAN'T CUT THE ENGINES, AND WE CAN'T USE MYSTIC MUMBO-JUMBO ENERGY. IF WE TRY TO STOP THE TRAIN BY BRUTE FORCE, WE'LL TEAR IT APART.
WHAT DOES THAT LEAVE?
I'LL TELL YE WHAT IT LEAVES!
YOU TWO NEED TO GET OFF THIS TRAIN BEFORE IT CRASHES!
HAVE THE PLANE PICK YE UP. I'M INDESTRUCTIBLE-- I'LL STAY HERE AN' TRY TO--
AREN'T YOU FORGETTING SOMETHING, LIAM?
"THERE'S A HUNDRED AND THIRTY PEOPLE ON THIS TRAIN.
"AND THEY'RE COUNTING ON US!"
ONE HUNDRED THIRTY-ONE, ACTUALLY.
A WOMAN IN THE LAST CAR JUST HAD A BABY.
HOW CAN YE KNOW THAT?!
TWITTER--
THE POINT IS: WE CAN'T JUST LEAVE ALL THESE PEOPLE TO DIE.

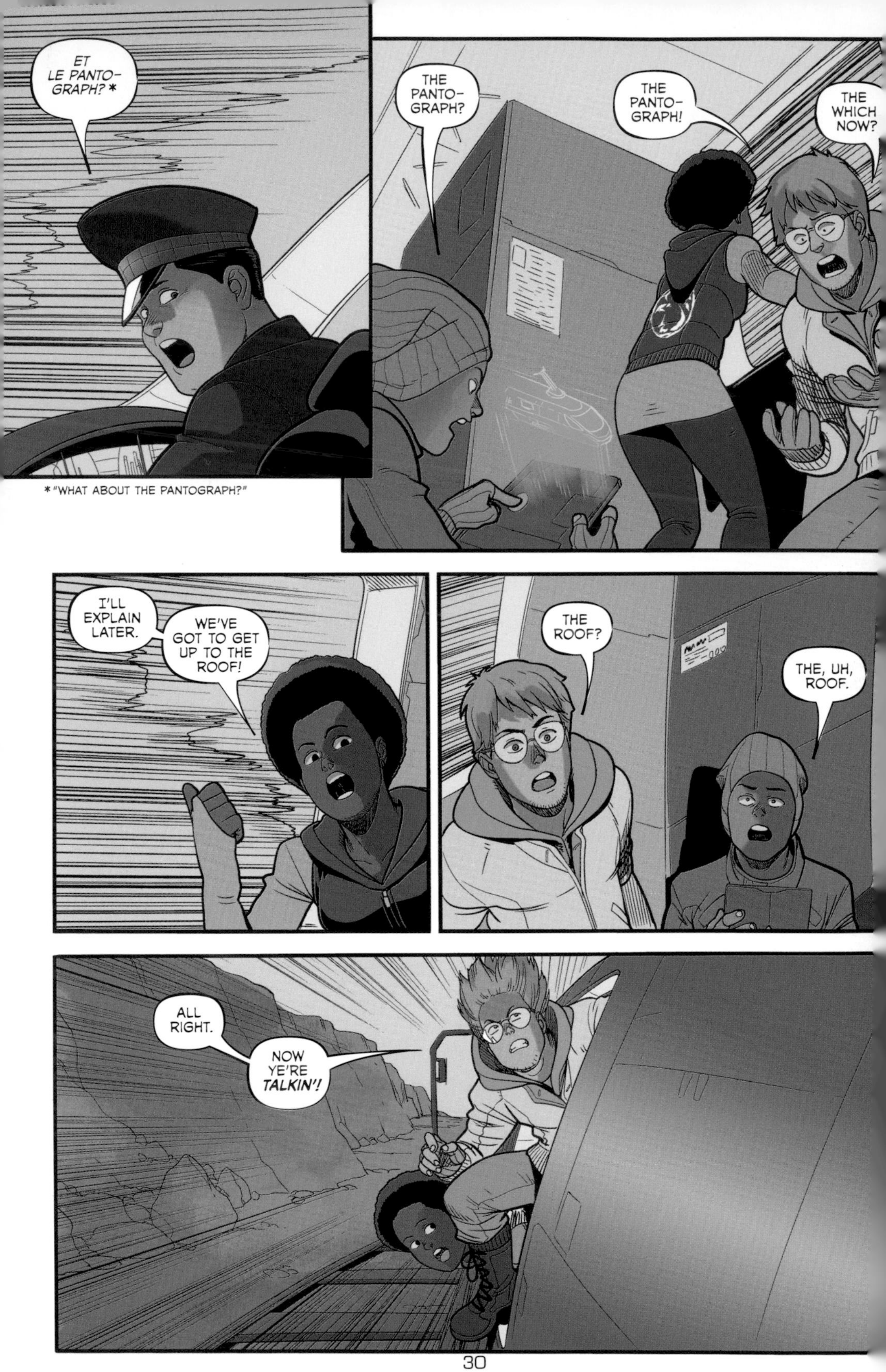
ET LE PANTOGRAPH? *
THE PANTOGRAPH?
THE PANTOGRAPH!
THE WHICH NOW?
I'LL EXPLAIN LATER.
WE'VE GOT TO GET UP TO THE ROOF!
THE ROOF?
THE, UH, ROOF.
ALL RIGHT.
NOW YE'RE *TALKIN'!*

* "WHAT ABOUT THE PANTOGRAPH?"

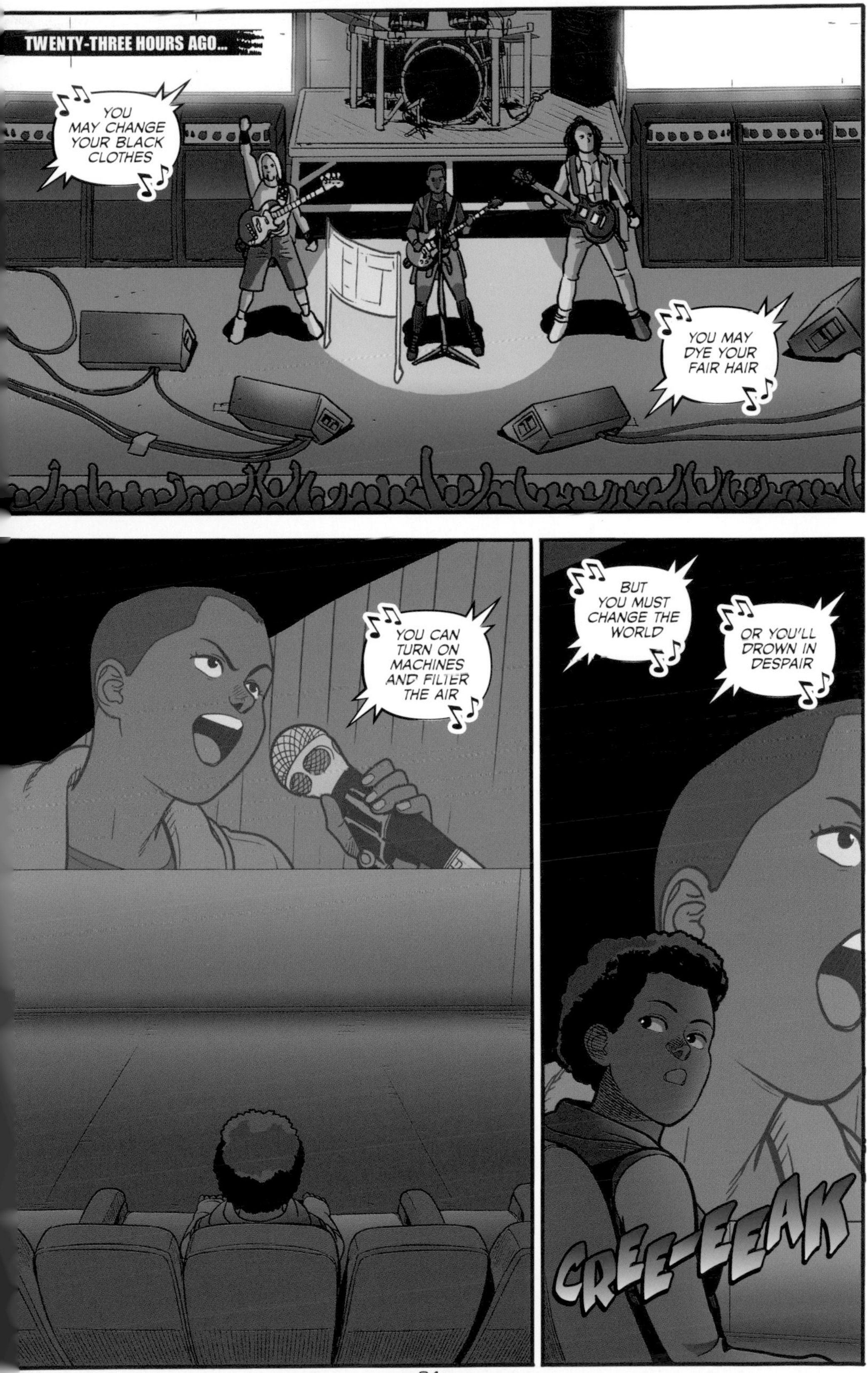
TWENTY-THREE HOURS AGO...
YOU MAY CHANGE YOUR BLACK CLOTHES
YOU MAY DYE YOUR FAIR HAIR
YOU CAN TURN ON MACHINES AND FILTER THE AIR
BUT YOU MUST CHANGE THE WORLD
OR YOU'LL DROWN IN DESPAIR
CREE-EEAK

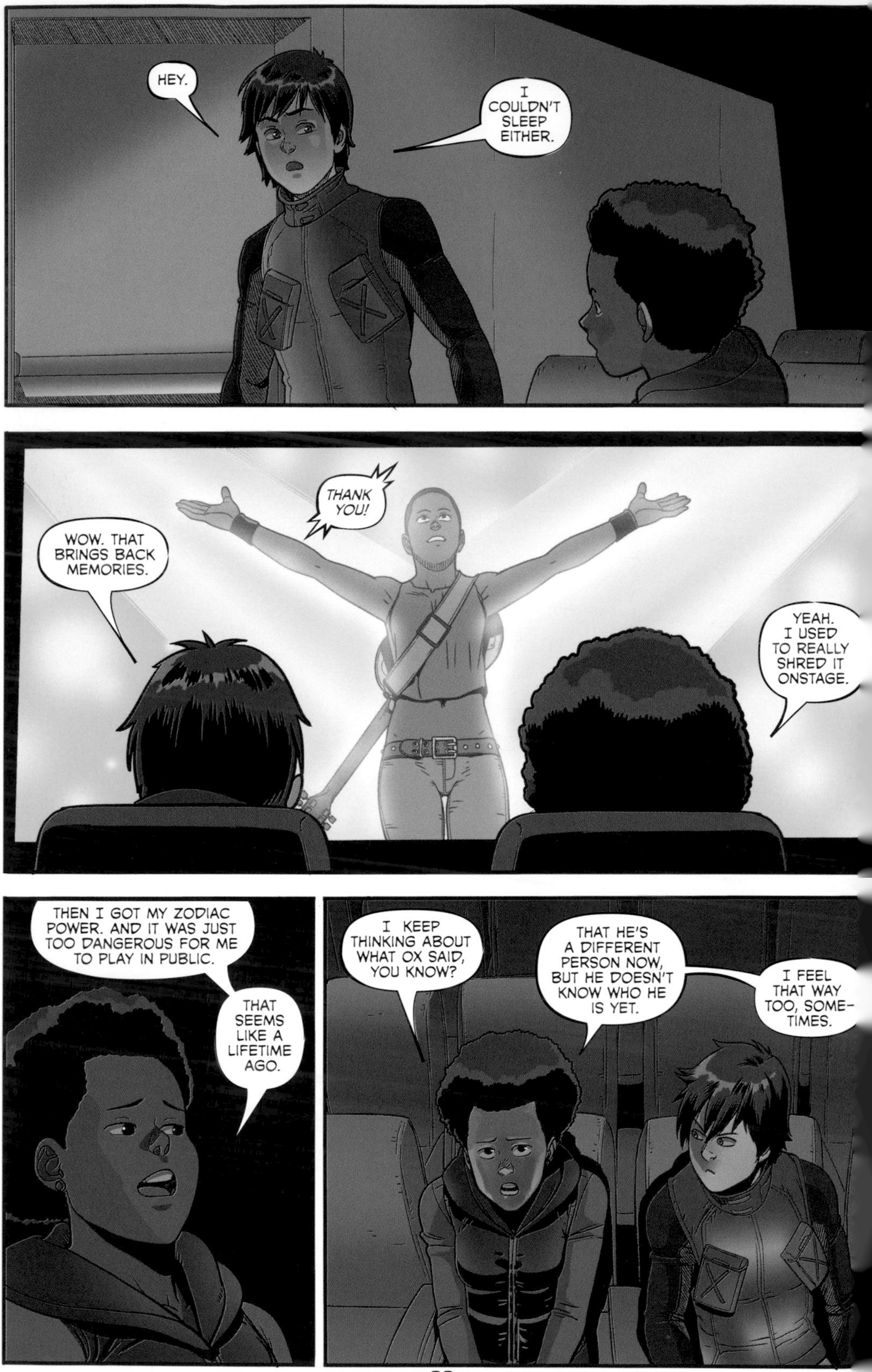
HEY.
I COULDN'T SLEEP EITHER.
THANK YOU!
WOW. THAT BRINGS BACK MEMORIES.
YEAH. I USED TO REALLY SHRED IT ONSTAGE.
THEN I GOT MY ZODIAC POWER. AND IT WAS JUST TOO DANGEROUS FOR ME TO PLAY IN PUBLIC.
THAT SEEMS LIKE A LIFETIME AGO.
I KEEP THINKING ABOUT WHAT OX SAID, YOU KNOW?
THAT HE'S A DIFFERENT PERSON NOW, BUT HE DOESN'T KNOW WHO HE IS YET.
I FEEL THAT WAY TOO, SOME-TIMES.

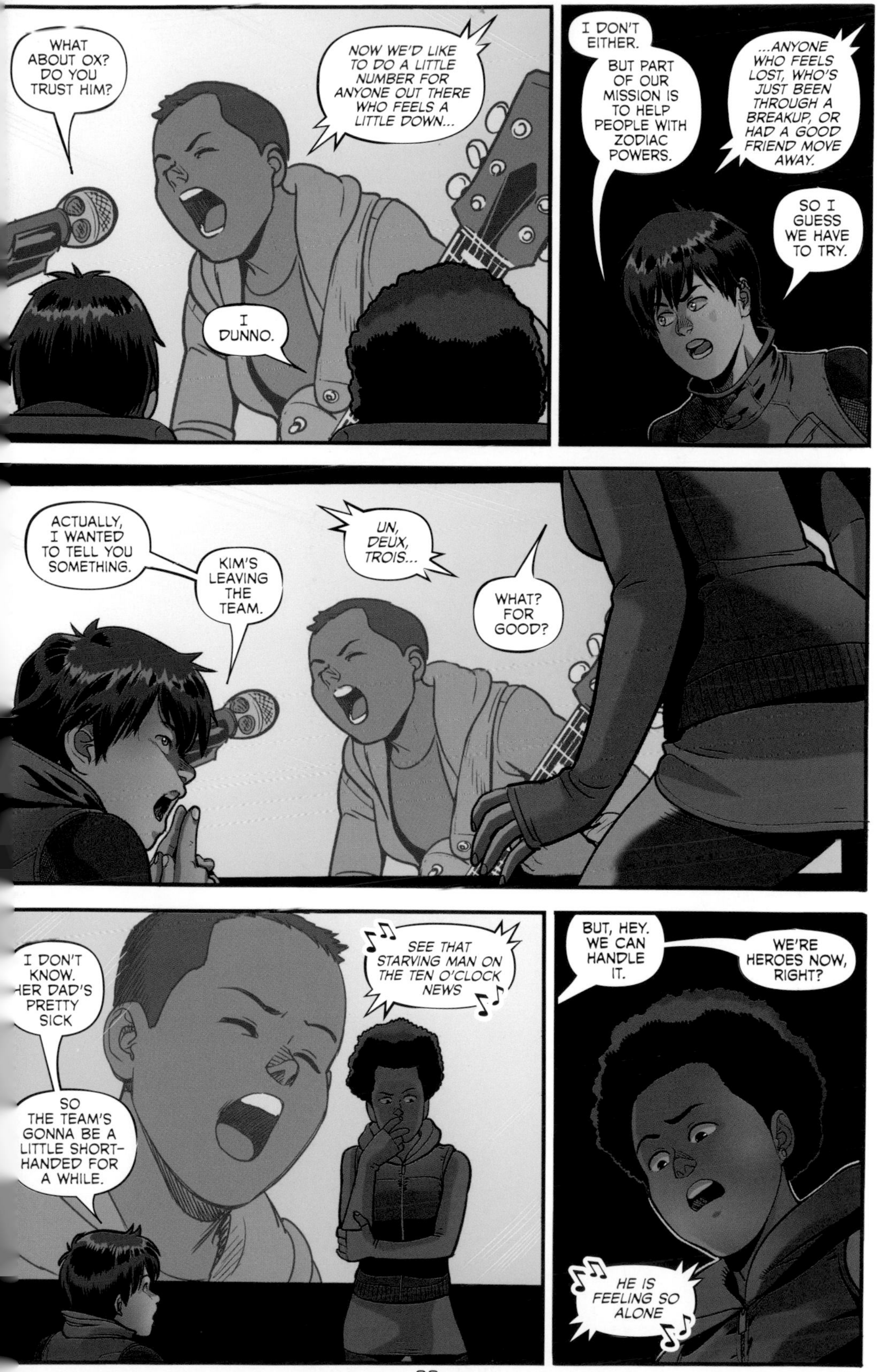
WHAT ABOUT OX? DO YOU TRUST HIM?
NOW WE'D LIKE TO DO A LITTLE NUMBER FOR ANYONE OUT THERE WHO FEELS A LITTLE DOWN...
I DUNNO.
I DON'T EITHER.
BUT PART OF OUR MISSION IS TO HELP PEOPLE WITH ZODIAC POWERS.
...ANYONE WHO FEELS LOST, WHO'S JUST BEEN THROUGH A BREAKUP, OR HAD A GOOD FRIEND MOVE AWAY.
SO I GUESS WE HAVE TO TRY.
ACTUALLY, I WANTED TO TELL YOU SOMETHING.
KIM'S LEAVING THE TEAM.
UN, DEUX, TROIS...
WHAT? FOR GOOD?
I DON'T KNOW. HER DAD'S PRETTY SICK
SO THE TEAM'S GONNA BE A LITTLE SHORT-HANDED FOR A WHILE.
SEE THAT STARVING MAN ON THE TEN O'CLOCK NEWS
BUT, HEY. WE CAN HANDLE IT.
WE'RE HEROES NOW, RIGHT?
HE IS FEELING SO ALONE

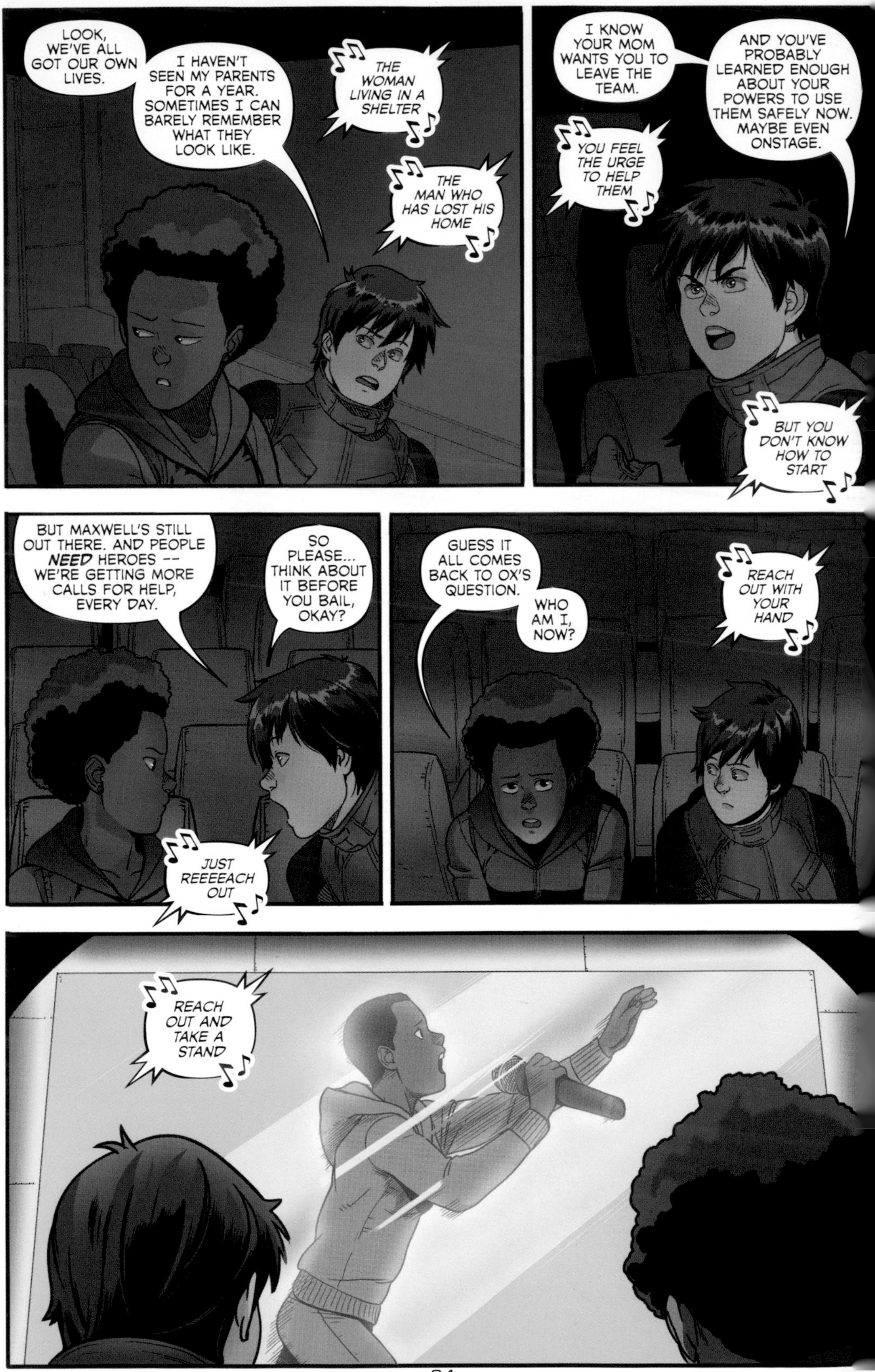

LOOK, WE'VE ALL GOT OUR OWN LIVES.
I HAVEN'T SEEN MY PARENTS FOR A YEAR. SOMETIMES I CAN BARELY REMEMBER WHAT THEY LOOK LIKE.
THE WOMAN LIVING IN A SHELTER
THE MAN WHO HAS LOST HIS HOME
I KNOW YOUR MOM WANTS YOU TO LEAVE THE TEAM.
AND YOU'VE PROBABLY LEARNED ENOUGH ABOUT YOUR POWERS TO USE THEM SAFELY NOW. MAYBE EVEN ONSTAGE.
YOU FEEL THE URGE TO HELP THEM
BUT YOU DON'T KNOW HOW TO START
BUT MAXWELL'S STILL OUT THERE. AND PEOPLE **NEED** HEROES -- WE'RE GETTING MORE CALLS FOR HELP, EVERY DAY.
SO PLEASE... THINK ABOUT IT BEFORE YOU BAIL, OKAY?
JUST REEEEACH OUT
GUESS IT ALL COMES BACK TO OX'S QUESTION.
WHO AM I, NOW?
REACH OUT WITH YOUR HAND
REACH OUT AND TAKE A STAND

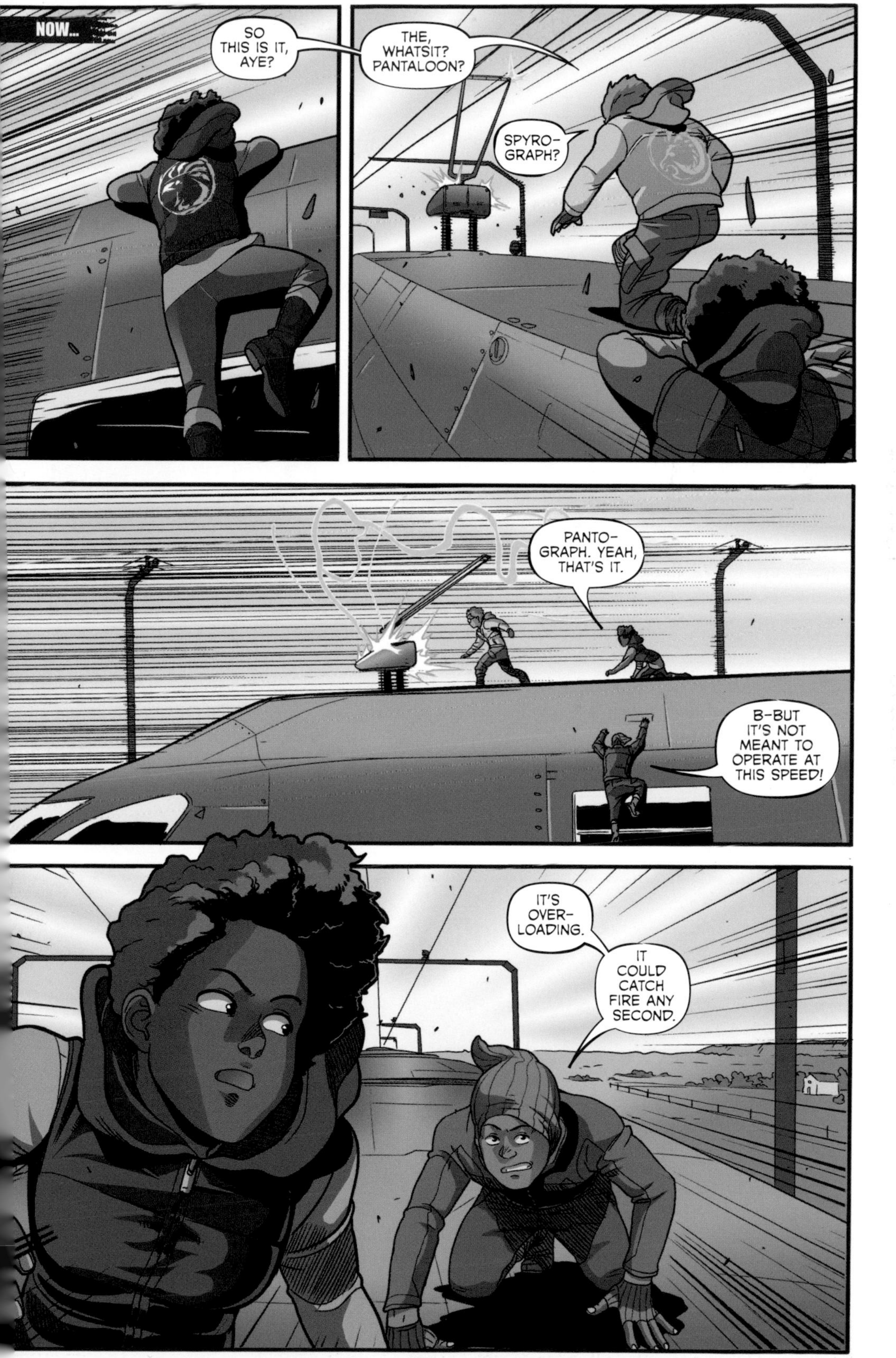
NOW...
SO THIS IS IT, AYE?
THE, WHATSIT? PANTALOON?
SPYRO-GRAPH?
PANTO-GRAPH. YEAH, THAT'S IT.
B-BUT IT'S NOT MEANT TO OPERATE AT THIS SPEED!
IT'S OVER-LOADING.
IT COULD CATCH FIRE ANY SECOND.

THE ENGINEER SAYS HE CAN'T REDUCE THE PANTOGRAPH TENSION FROM INSIDE.

THE CONTROLS ARE COMPLETELY FUSED.

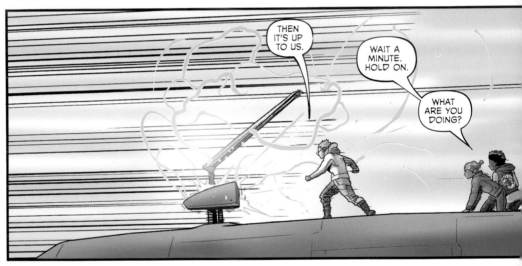

THEN IT'S UP TO US.

WAIT A MINUTE. HOLD ON.

WHAT ARE YOU DOING?

I'M GONNA *RAM* IT.

D-DID I MENTION THAT WIRE HAS OVER NINE HUNDRED VOLTS RUNNING THROUGH IT?

ARE YOU CLINICALLY INSANE?

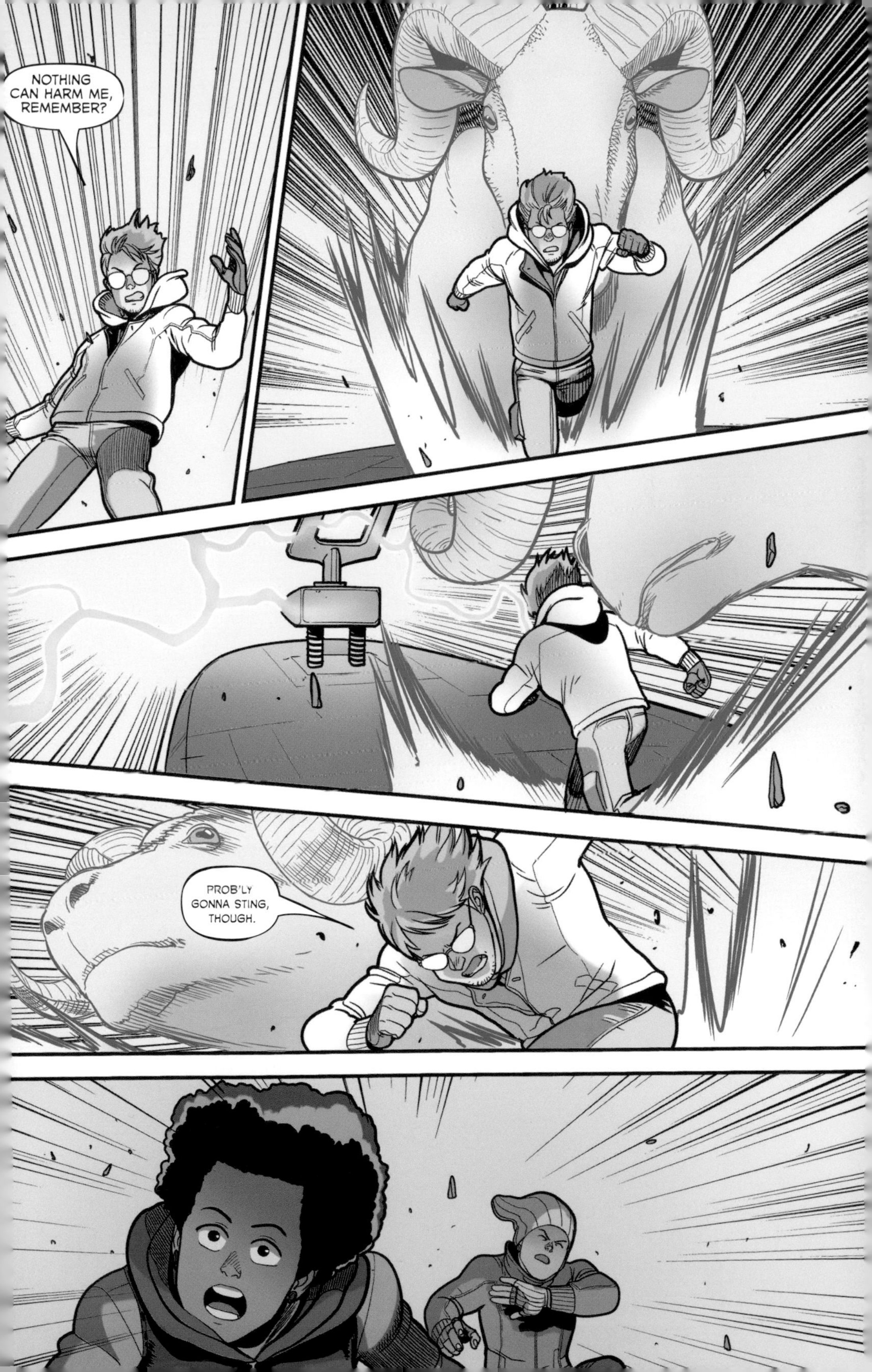
NOTHING CAN HARM ME, REMEMBER?
PROB'LY GONNA STING, THOUGH.

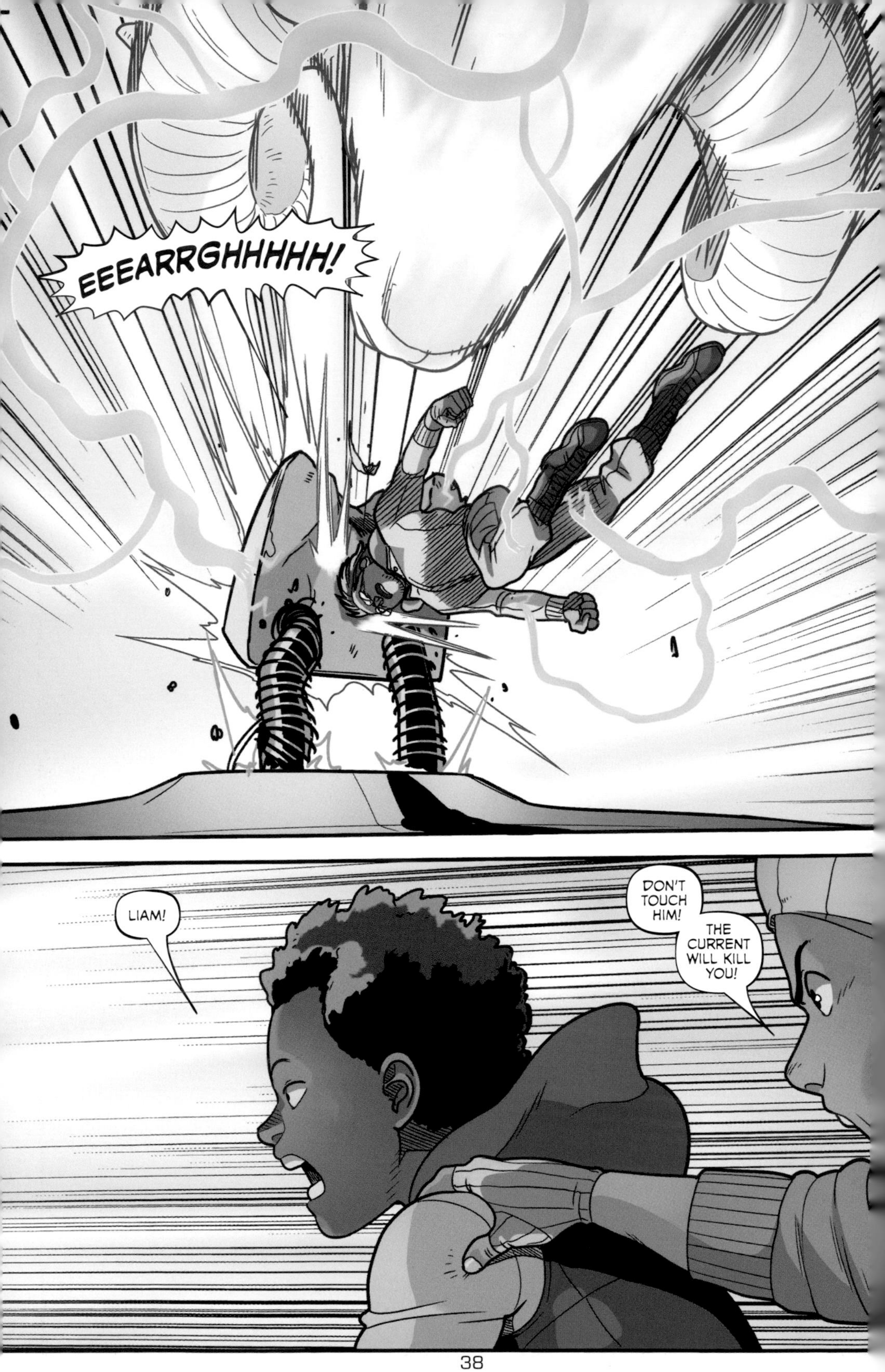
EEEARRGHHHHH!
LIAM!
DON'T TOUCH HIM!
THE CURRENT WILL KILL YOU!

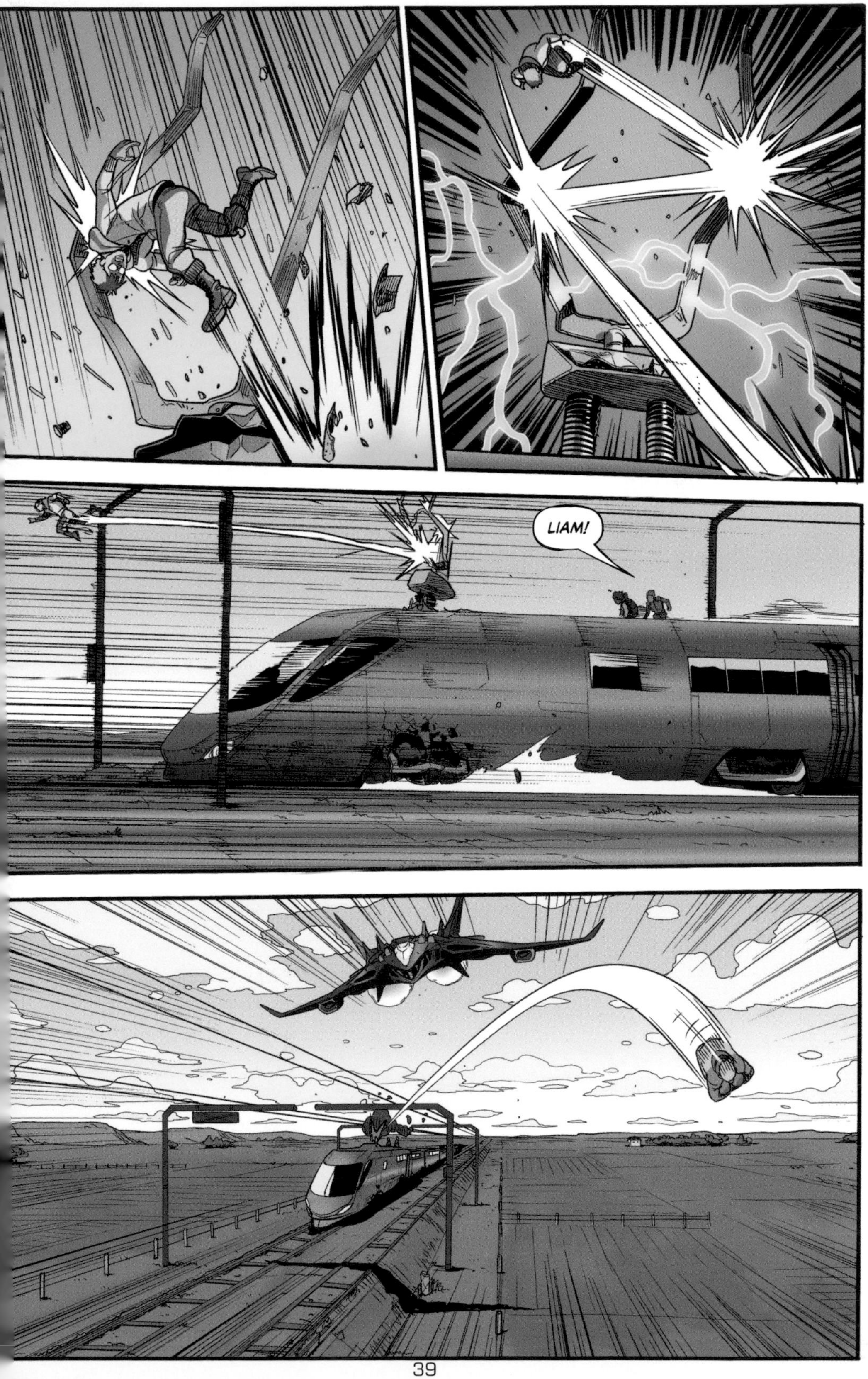
LIAM!

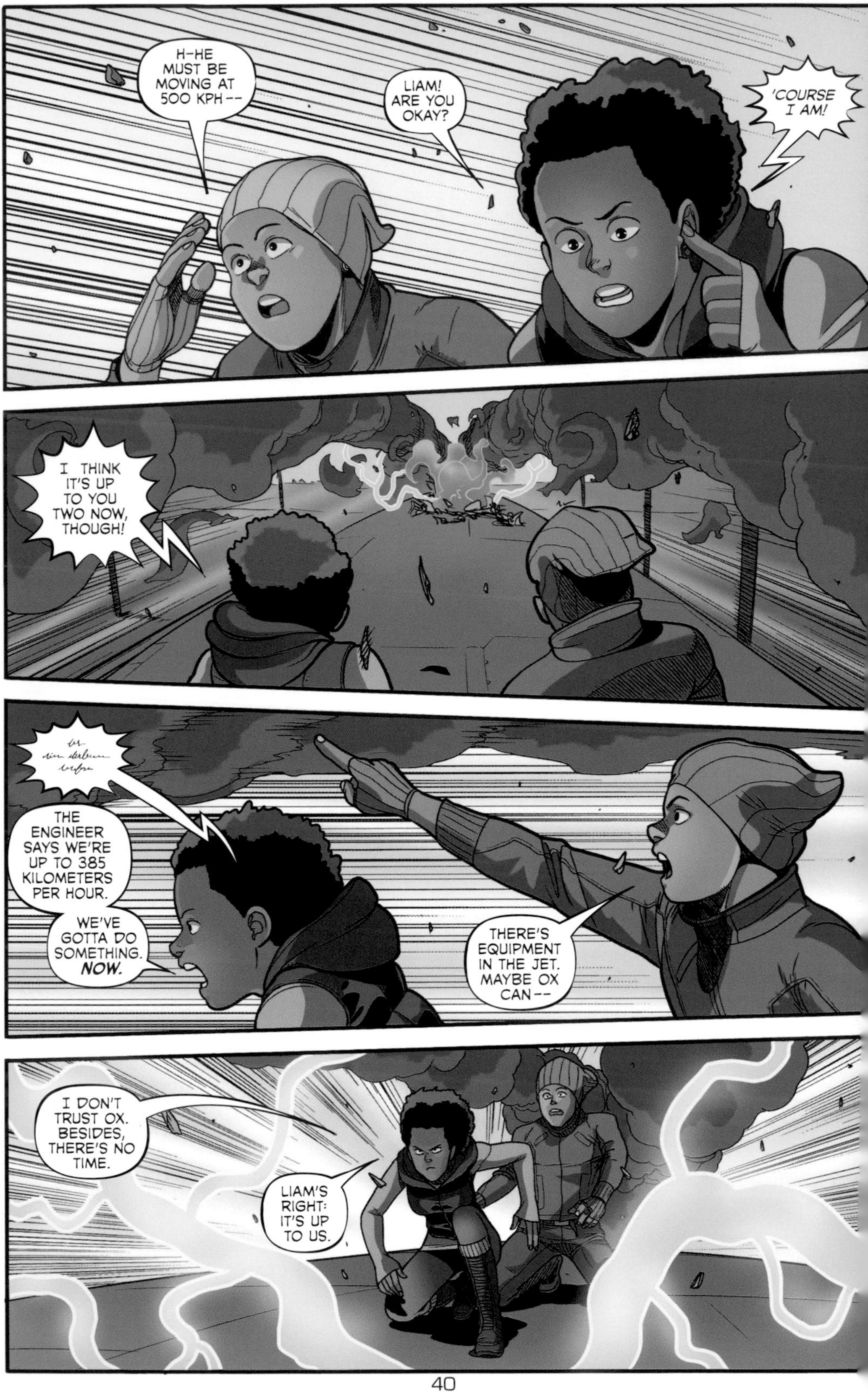
H-HE MUST BE MOVING AT 500 KPH--
LIAM! ARE YOU OKAY?
'COURSE I AM!
I THINK IT'S UP TO YOU TWO NOW, THOUGH!
THE ENGINEER SAYS WE'RE UP TO 385 KILOMETERS PER HOUR.
WE'VE GOTTA DO SOMETHING. ***NOW.***
THERE'S EQUIPMENT IN THE JET. MAYBE OX CAN--
I DON'T TRUST OX. BESIDES, THERE'S NO TIME.
LIAM'S RIGHT: IT'S UP TO US.

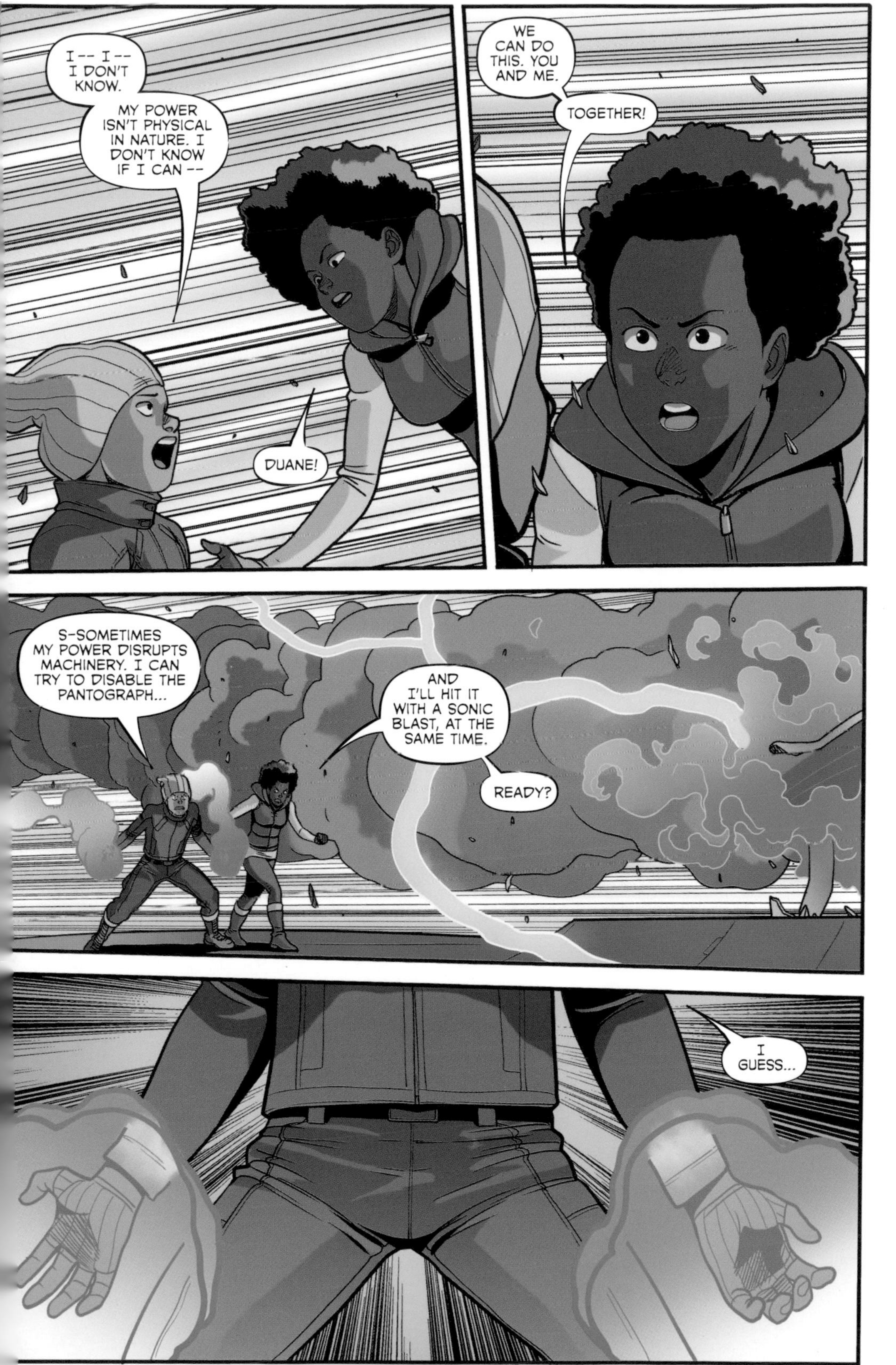
I -- I -- I DON'T KNOW.
MY POWER ISN'T PHYSICAL IN NATURE. I DON'T KNOW IF I CAN --
DUANE!
WE CAN DO THIS. YOU AND ME.
TOGETHER!
S-SOMETIMES MY POWER DISRUPTS MACHINERY. I CAN TRY TO DISABLE THE PANTOGRAPH...
AND I'LL HIT IT WITH A SONIC BLAST, AT THE SAME TIME.
READY?
I GUESS...

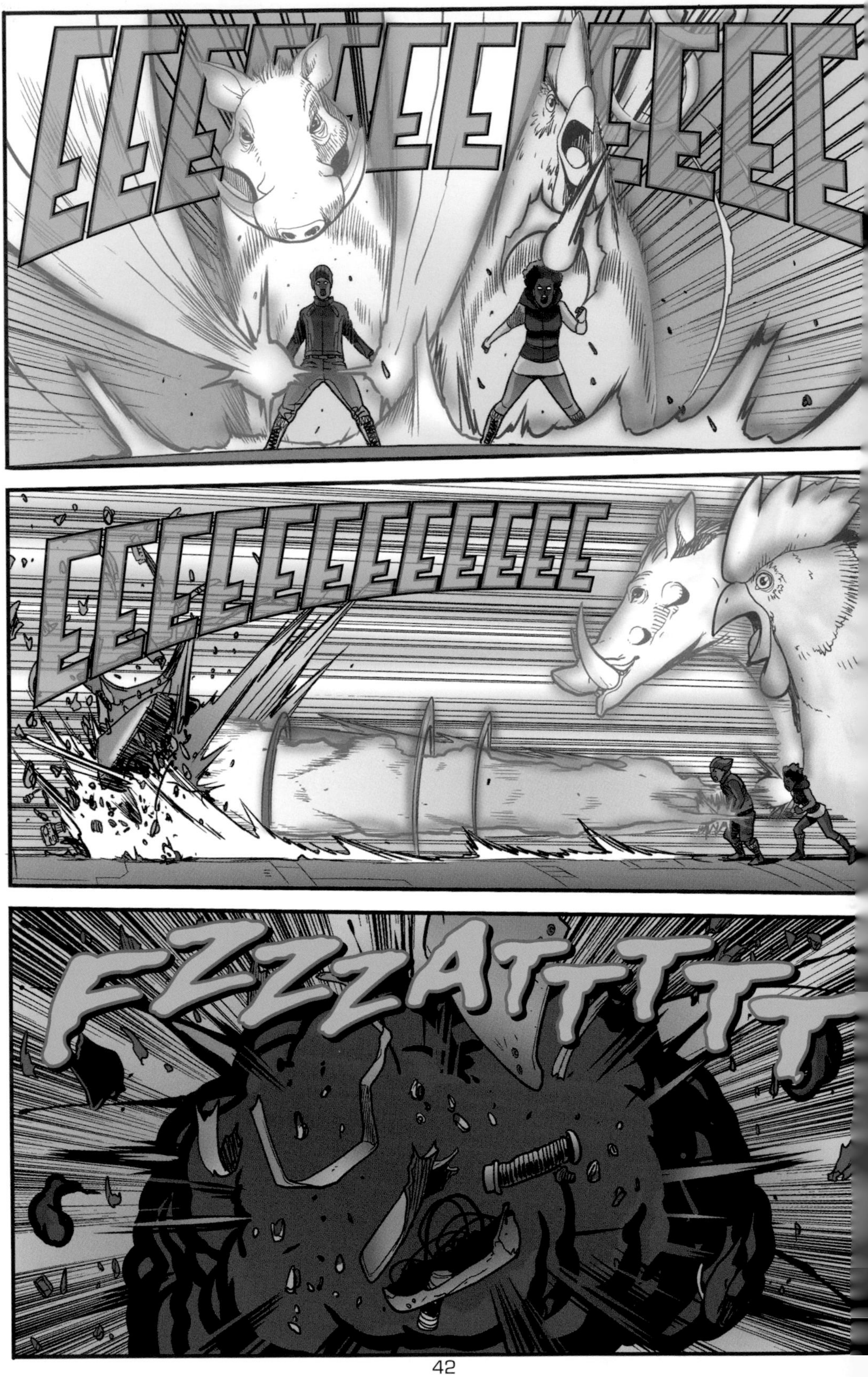
EEEEEEEEEEEEE
EEEEEEEEEEE
FZZZATTTTT

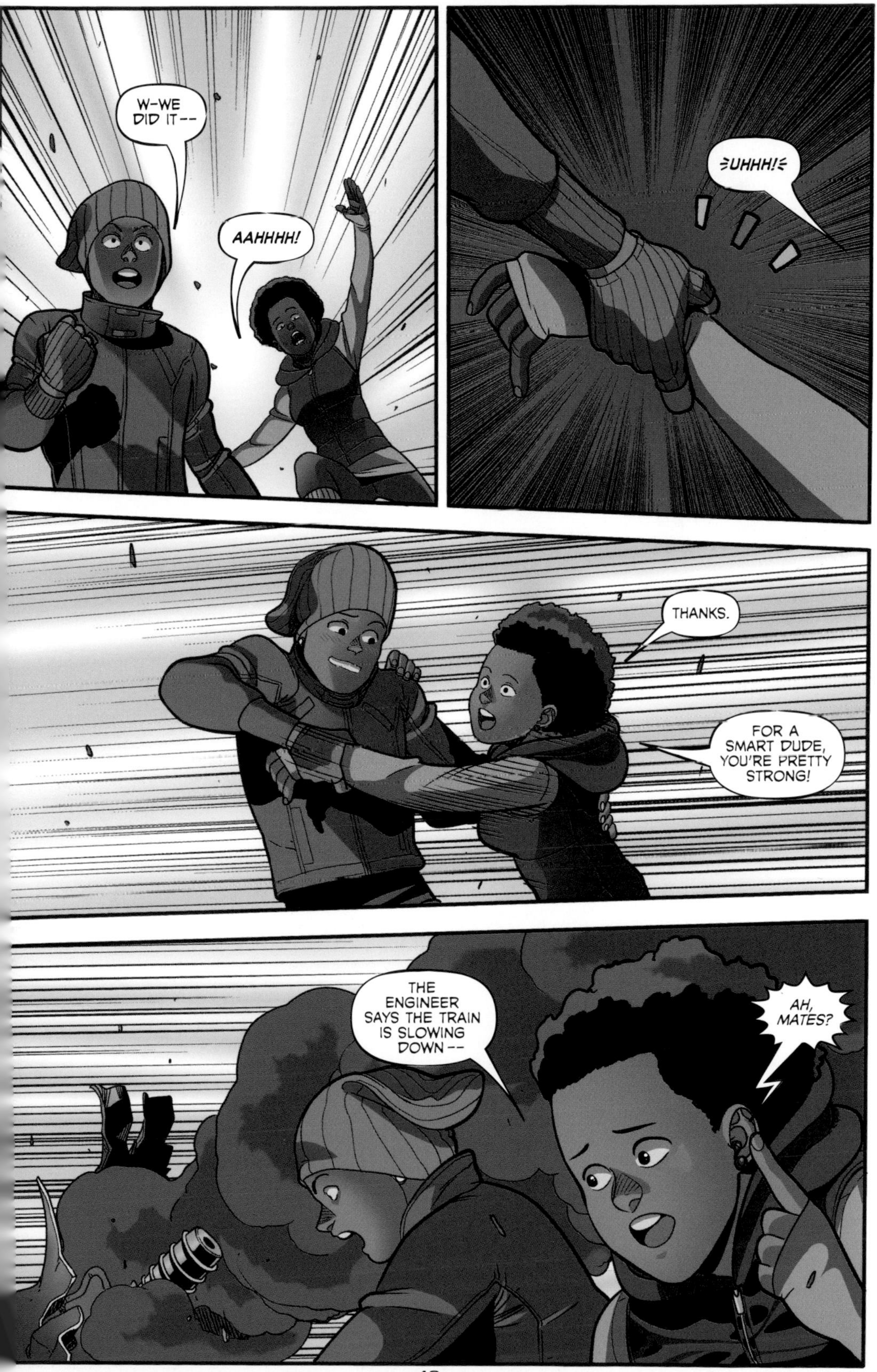
W-WE DID IT--
AAHHHH!
UHHH!
THANKS.
FOR A SMART DUDE, YOU'RE PRETTY STRONG!
THE ENGINEER SAYS THE TRAIN IS SLOWING DOWN--
AH, MATES?

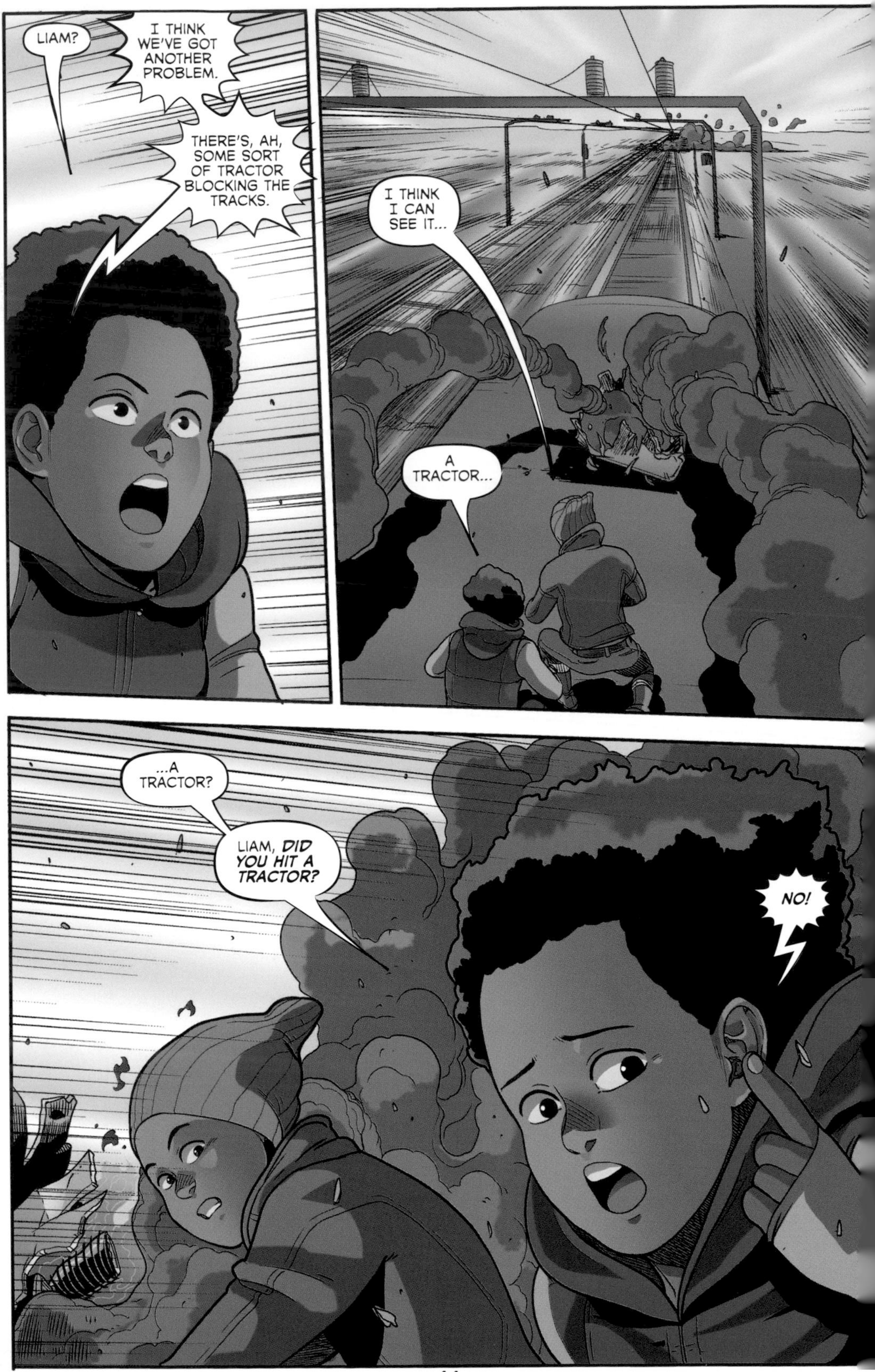
LIAM?
I THINK WE'VE GOT ANOTHER PROBLEM.
THERE'S, AH, SOME SORT OF TRACTOR BLOCKING THE TRACKS.
I THINK I CAN SEE IT...
A TRACTOR...
...A TRACTOR?
LIAM, *DID YOU HIT A TRACTOR?*
NO!

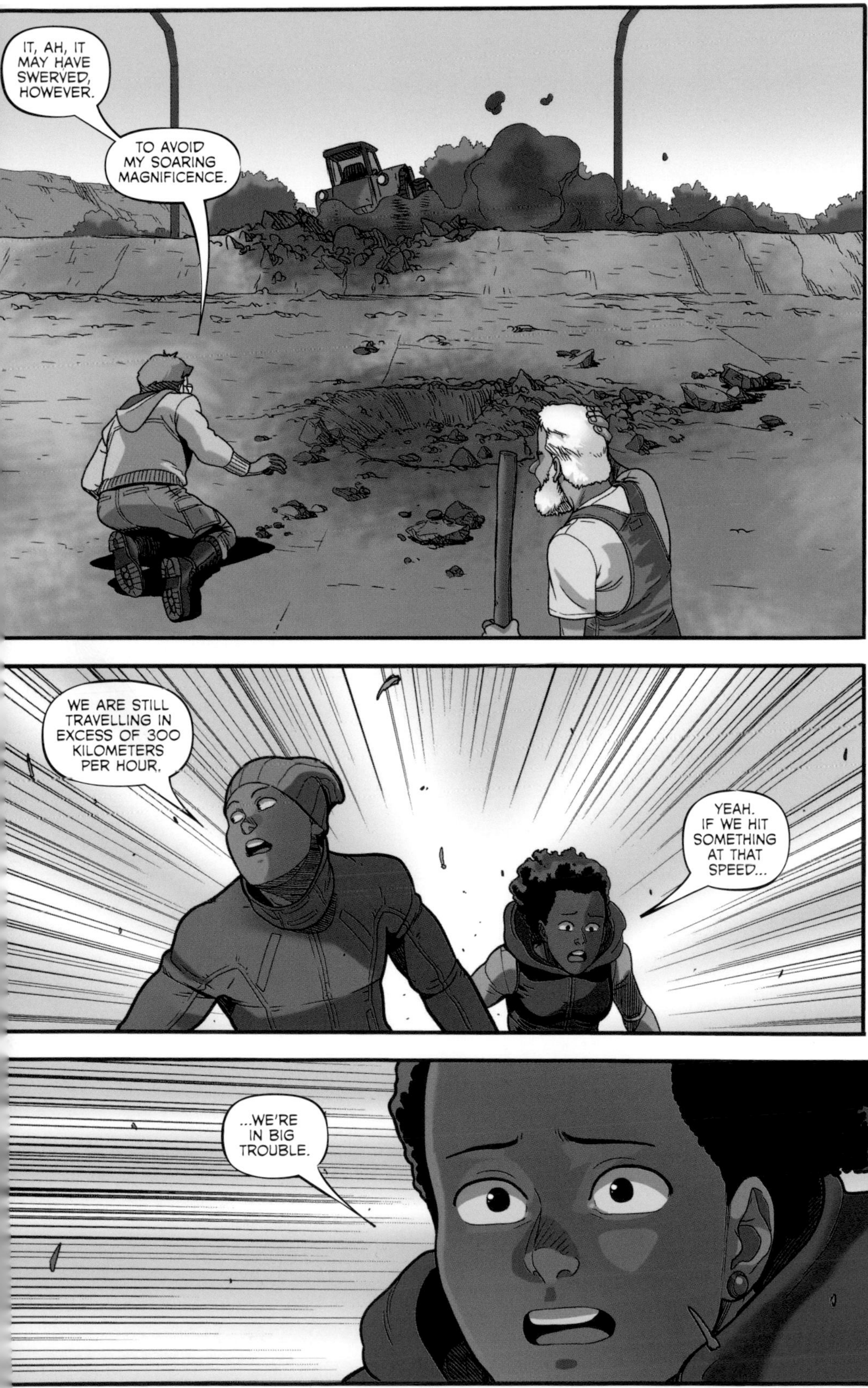
IT, AH, IT MAY HAVE SWERVED, HOWEVER.
TO AVOID MY SOARING MAGNIFICENCE.
WE ARE STILL TRAVELLING IN EXCESS OF 300 KILOMETERS PER HOUR,
YEAH. IF WE HIT SOMETHING AT THAT SPEED...
...WE'RE IN BIG TROUBLE.

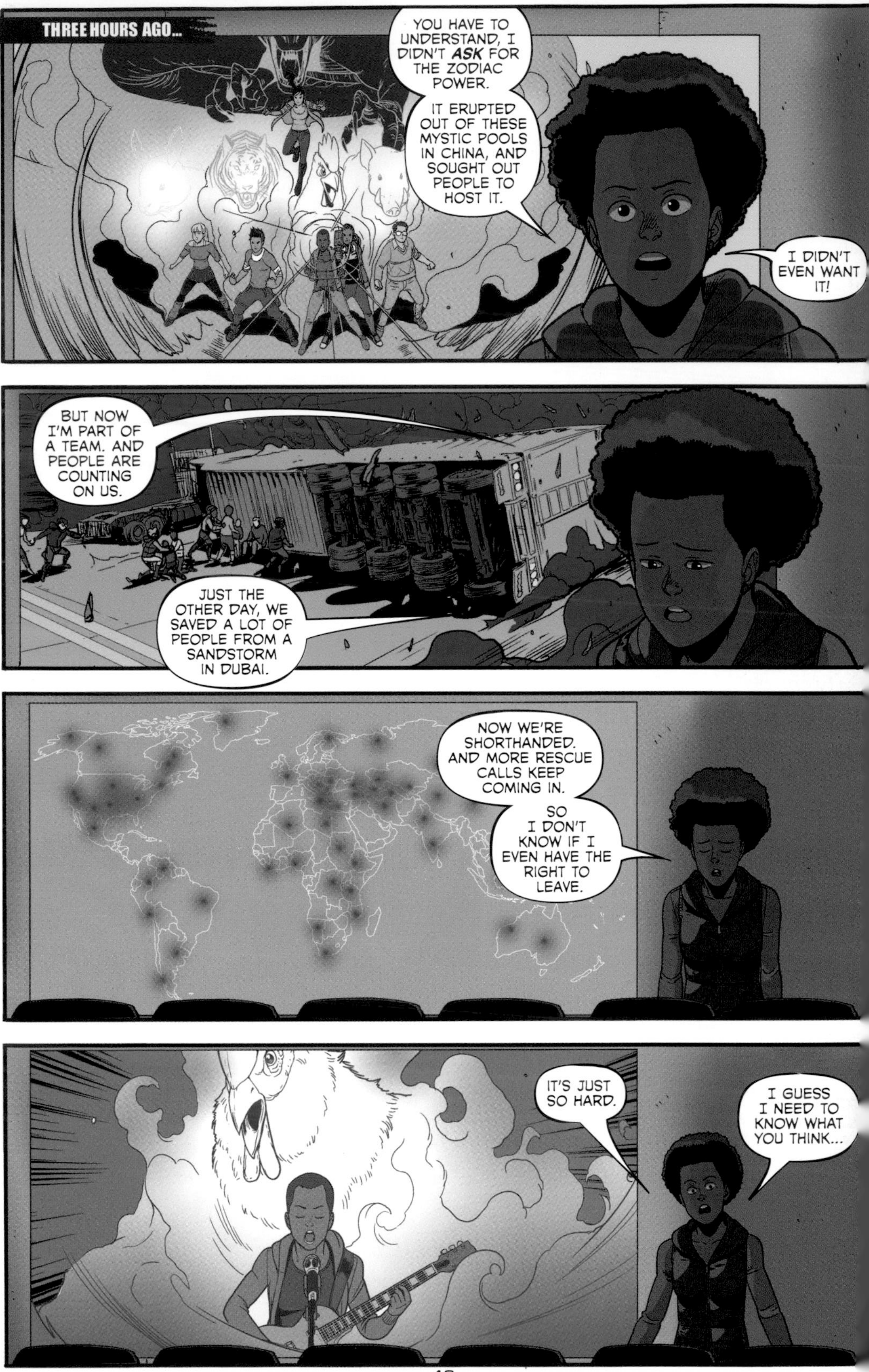
THREE HOURS AGO...
YOU HAVE TO UNDERSTAND, I DIDN'T ASK FOR THE ZODIAC POWER.
IT ERUPTED OUT OF THESE MYSTIC POOLS IN CHINA, AND SOUGHT OUT PEOPLE TO HOST IT.
I DIDN'T EVEN WANT IT!
BUT NOW I'M PART OF A TEAM. AND PEOPLE ARE COUNTING ON US.
JUST THE OTHER DAY, WE SAVED A LOT OF PEOPLE FROM A SANDSTORM IN DUBAI.
NOW WE'RE SHORTHANDED. AND MORE RESCUE CALLS KEEP COMING IN.
SO I DON'T KNOW IF I EVEN HAVE THE RIGHT TO LEAVE.
IT'S JUST SO HARD.
I GUESS I NEED TO KNOW WHAT YOU THINK...

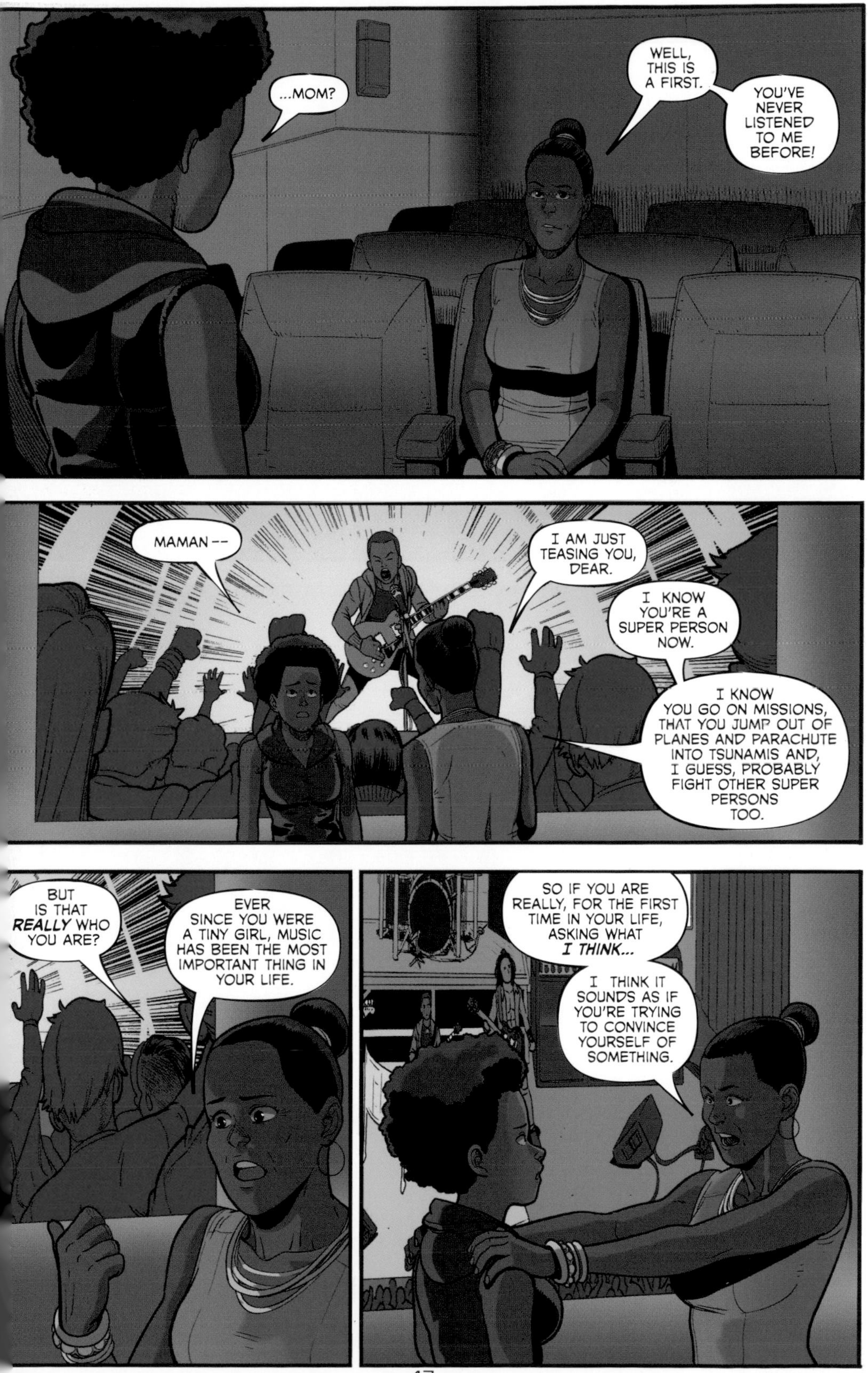
...MOM?
WELL, THIS IS A FIRST.
YOU'VE NEVER LISTENED TO ME BEFORE!
MAMAN --
I AM JUST TEASING YOU, DEAR.
I KNOW YOU'RE A SUPER PERSON NOW.
I KNOW YOU GO ON MISSIONS, THAT YOU JUMP OUT OF PLANES AND PARACHUTE INTO TSUNAMIS AND, I GUESS, PROBABLY FIGHT OTHER SUPER PERSONS TOO.
BUT IS THAT *REALLY* WHO YOU ARE?
EVER SINCE YOU WERE A TINY GIRL, MUSIC HAS BEEN THE MOST IMPORTANT THING IN YOUR LIFE.
SO IF YOU ARE REALLY, FOR THE FIRST TIME IN YOUR LIFE, ASKING WHAT *I THINK...*
I THINK IT SOUNDS AS IF YOU'RE TRYING TO CONVINCE YOURSELF OF SOMETHING.

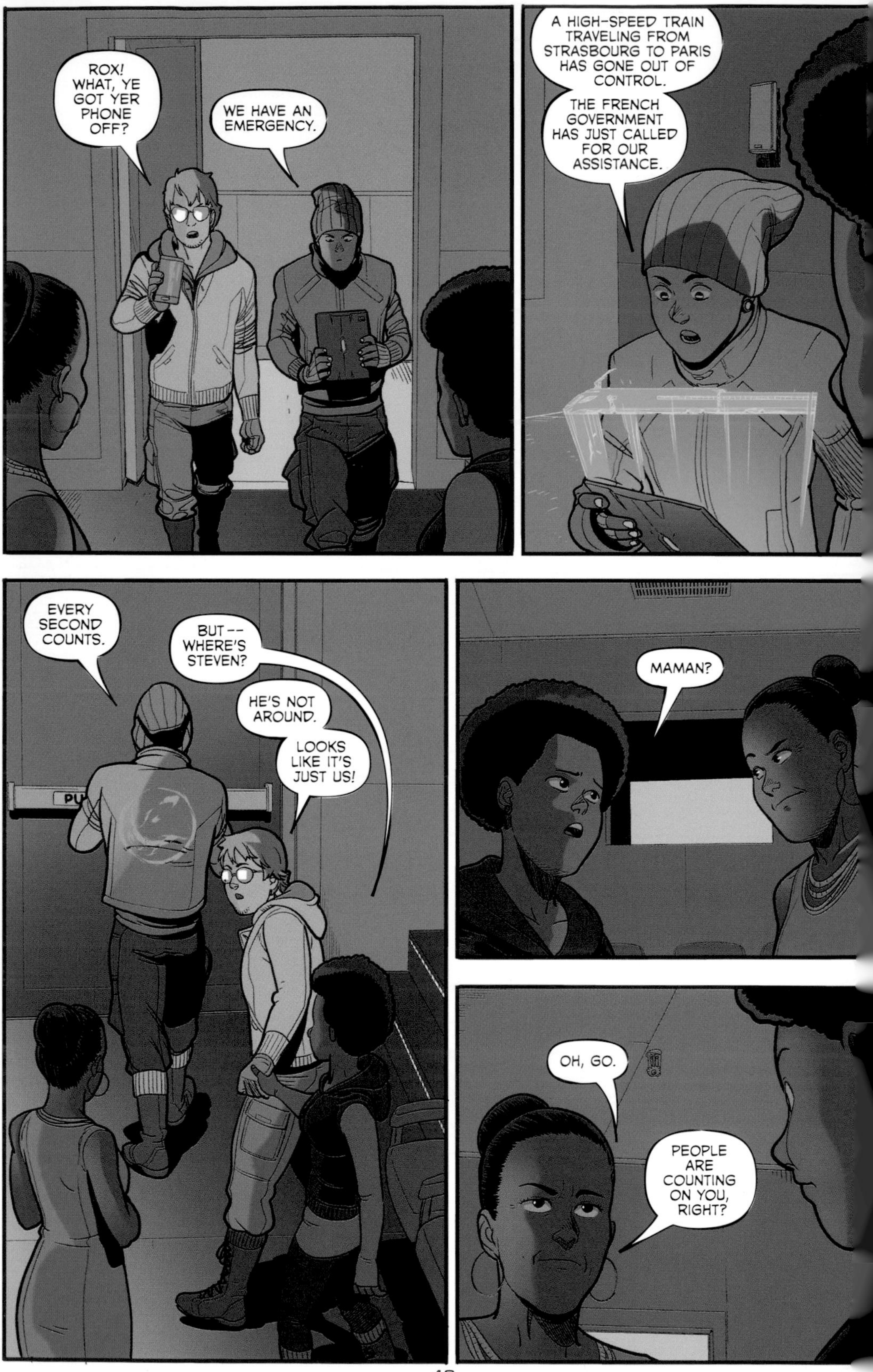
ROX! WHAT, YE GOT YER PHONE OFF?
WE HAVE AN EMERGENCY.
A HIGH-SPEED TRAIN TRAVELING FROM STRASBOURG TO PARIS HAS GONE OUT OF CONTROL.
THE FRENCH GOVERNMENT HAS JUST CALLED FOR OUR ASSISTANCE.
EVERY SECOND COUNTS.
BUT-- WHERE'S STEVEN?
HE'S NOT AROUND.
LOOKS LIKE IT'S JUST US!
MAMAN?
OH, GO.
PEOPLE ARE COUNTING ON YOU, RIGHT?

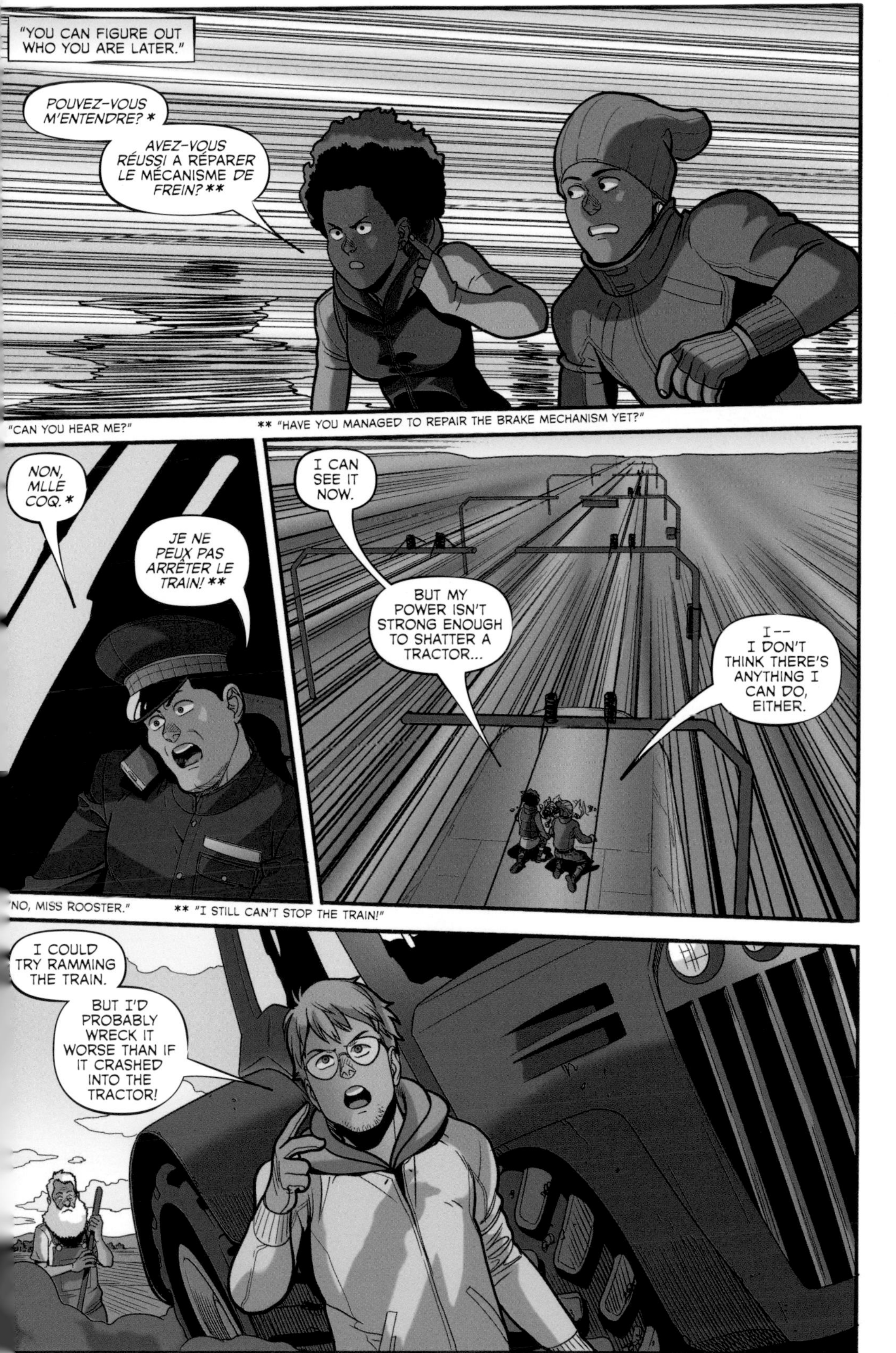
"YOU CAN FIGURE OUT WHO YOU ARE LATER."
POUVEZ-VOUS M'ENTENDRE? *
AVEZ-VOUS RÉUSSI A RÉPARER LE MÉCANISME DE FREIN? **
* "CAN YOU HEAR ME?"
** "HAVE YOU MANAGED TO REPAIR THE BRAKE MECHANISM YET?"
NON, MLLE COQ. *
JE NE PEUX PAS ARRÊTER LE TRAIN! **
I CAN SEE IT NOW.
BUT MY POWER ISN'T STRONG ENOUGH TO SHATTER A TRACTOR...
I-- I DON'T THINK THERE'S ANYTHING I CAN DO, EITHER.
* "NO, MISS ROOSTER."
** "I STILL CAN'T STOP THE TRAIN!"
I COULD TRY RAMMING THE TRAIN.
BUT I'D PROBABLY WRECK IT WORSE THAN IF IT CRASHED INTO THE TRACTOR!

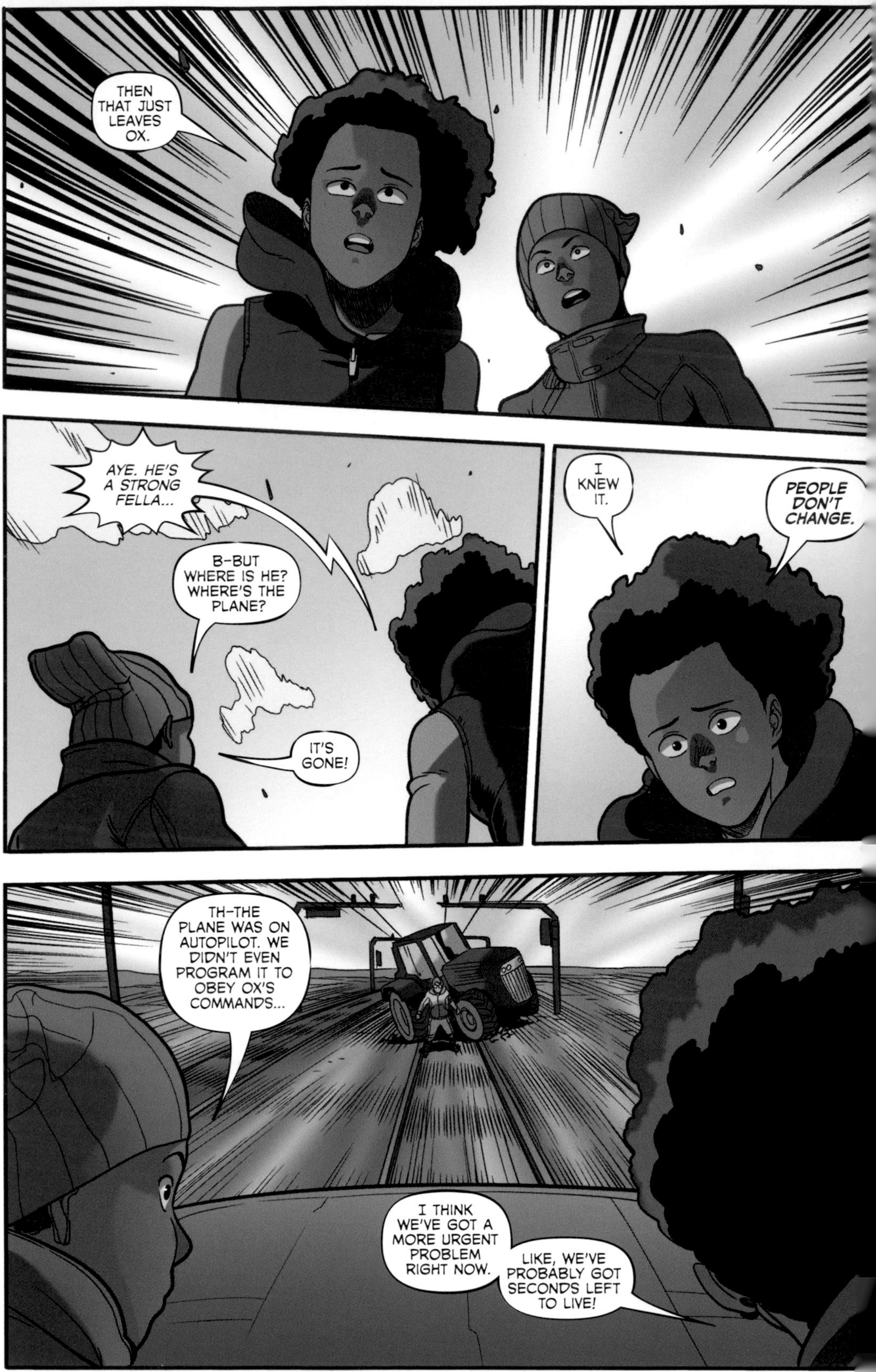
THEN THAT JUST LEAVES OX.
AYE. HE'S A STRONG FELLA...
B-BUT WHERE IS HE? WHERE'S THE PLANE?
IT'S GONE!
I KNEW IT.
PEOPLE DON'T CHANGE.
TH-THE PLANE WAS ON AUTOPILOT. WE DIDN'T EVEN PROGRAM IT TO OBEY OX'S COMMANDS...
I THINK WE'VE GOT A MORE URGENT PROBLEM RIGHT NOW.
LIKE, WE'VE PROBABLY GOT SECONDS LEFT TO LIVE!

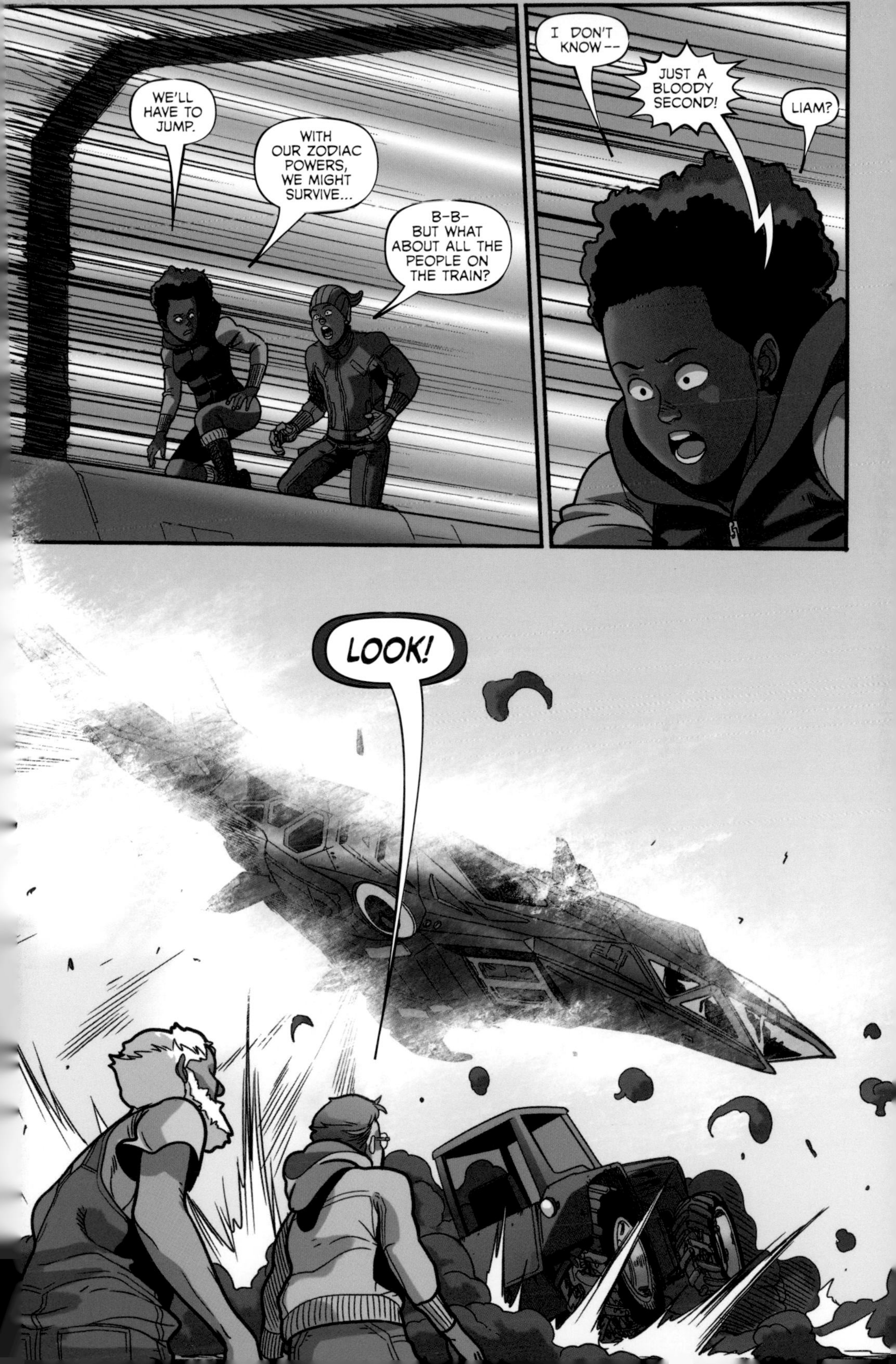
WE'LL HAVE TO JUMP.
WITH OUR ZODIAC POWERS, WE MIGHT SURVIVE...
B-B- BUT WHAT ABOUT ALL THE PEOPLE ON THE TRAIN?
I DON'T KNOW--
JUST A BLOODY SECOND!
LIAM?
LOOK!

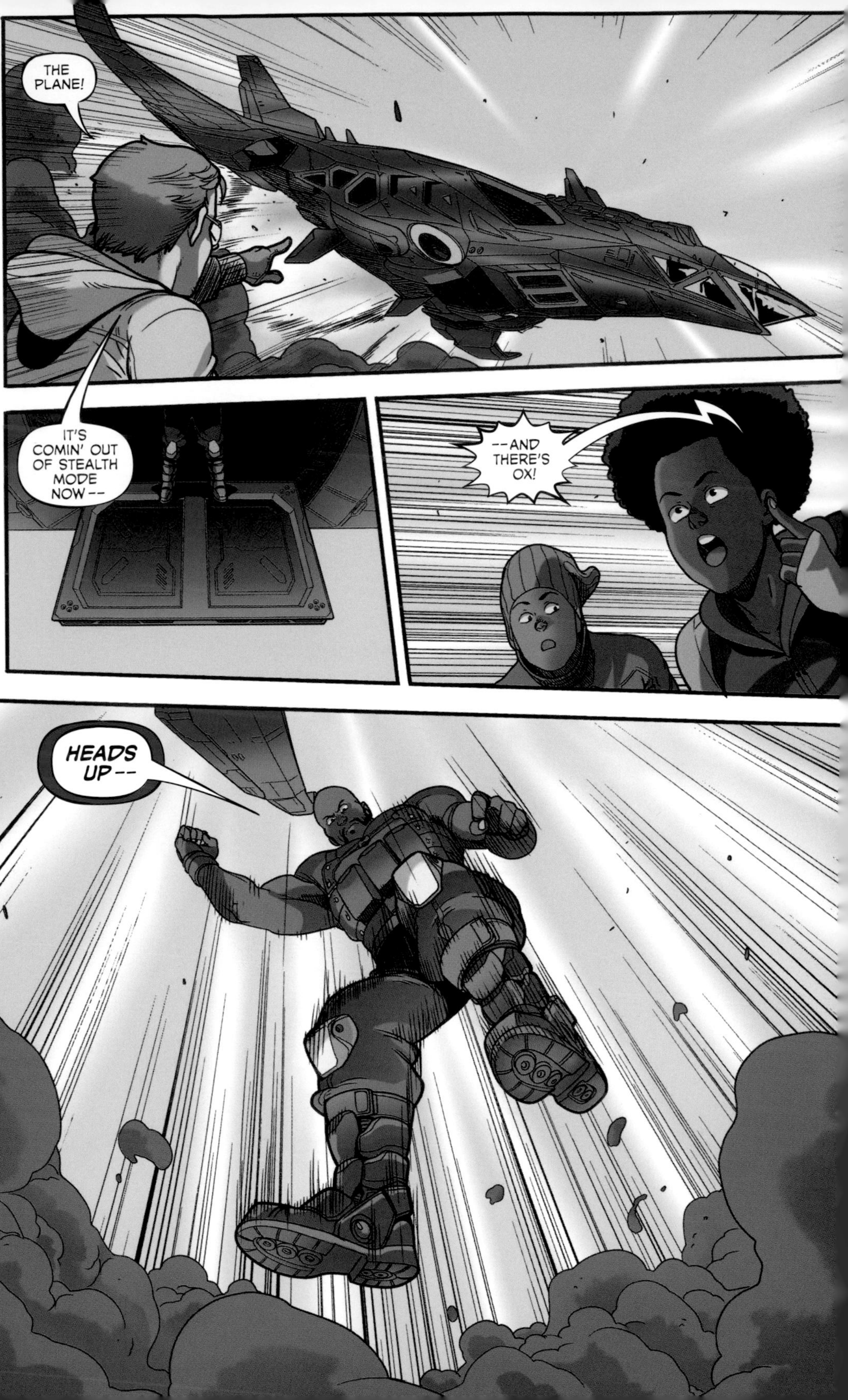
THE PLANE!
IT'S COMIN' OUT OF STEALTH MODE NOW --
--AND THERE'S OX!
HEADS UP --

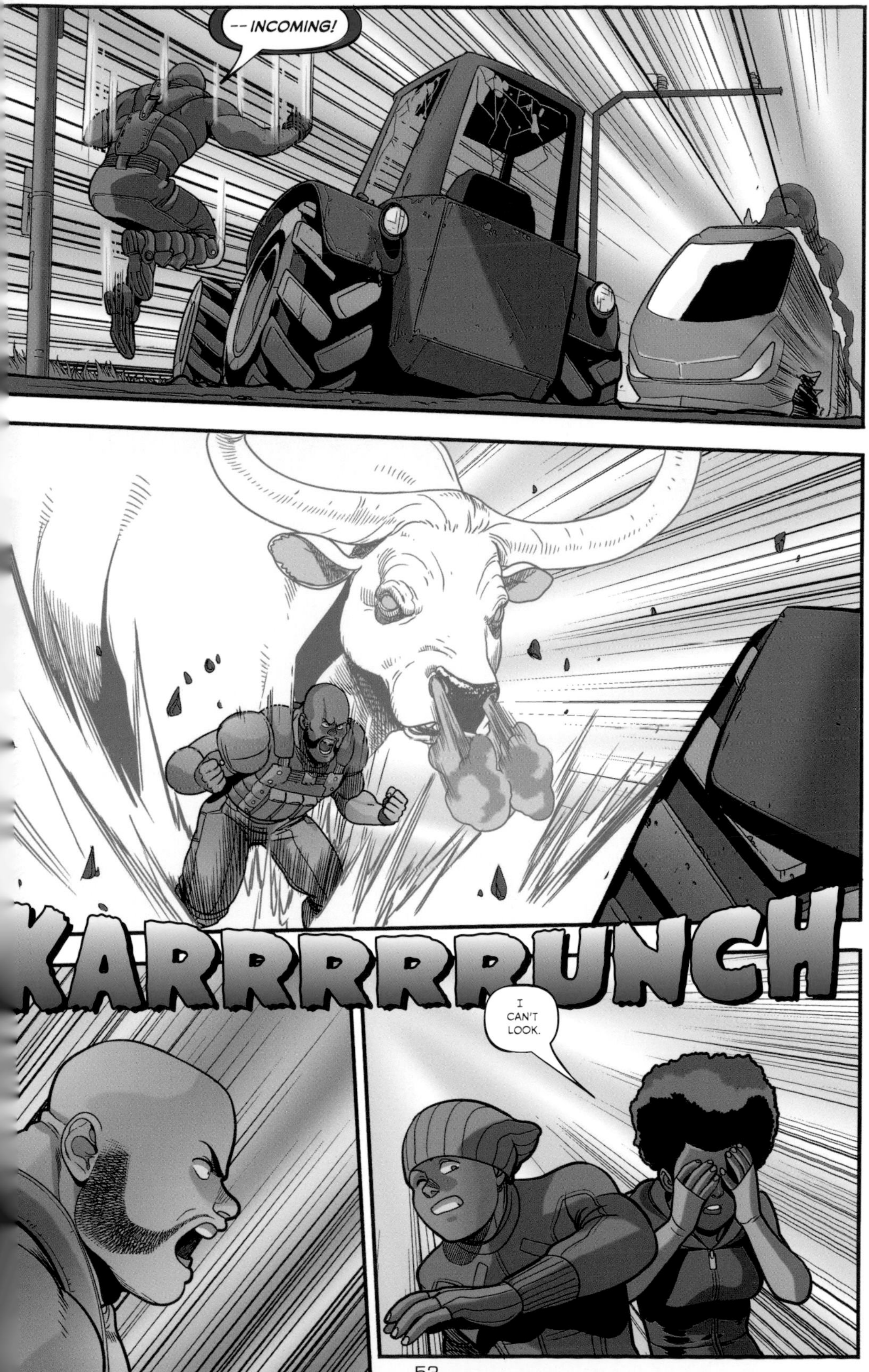
--INCOMING!
KARRRRRRUNCH
I CAN'T LOOK.

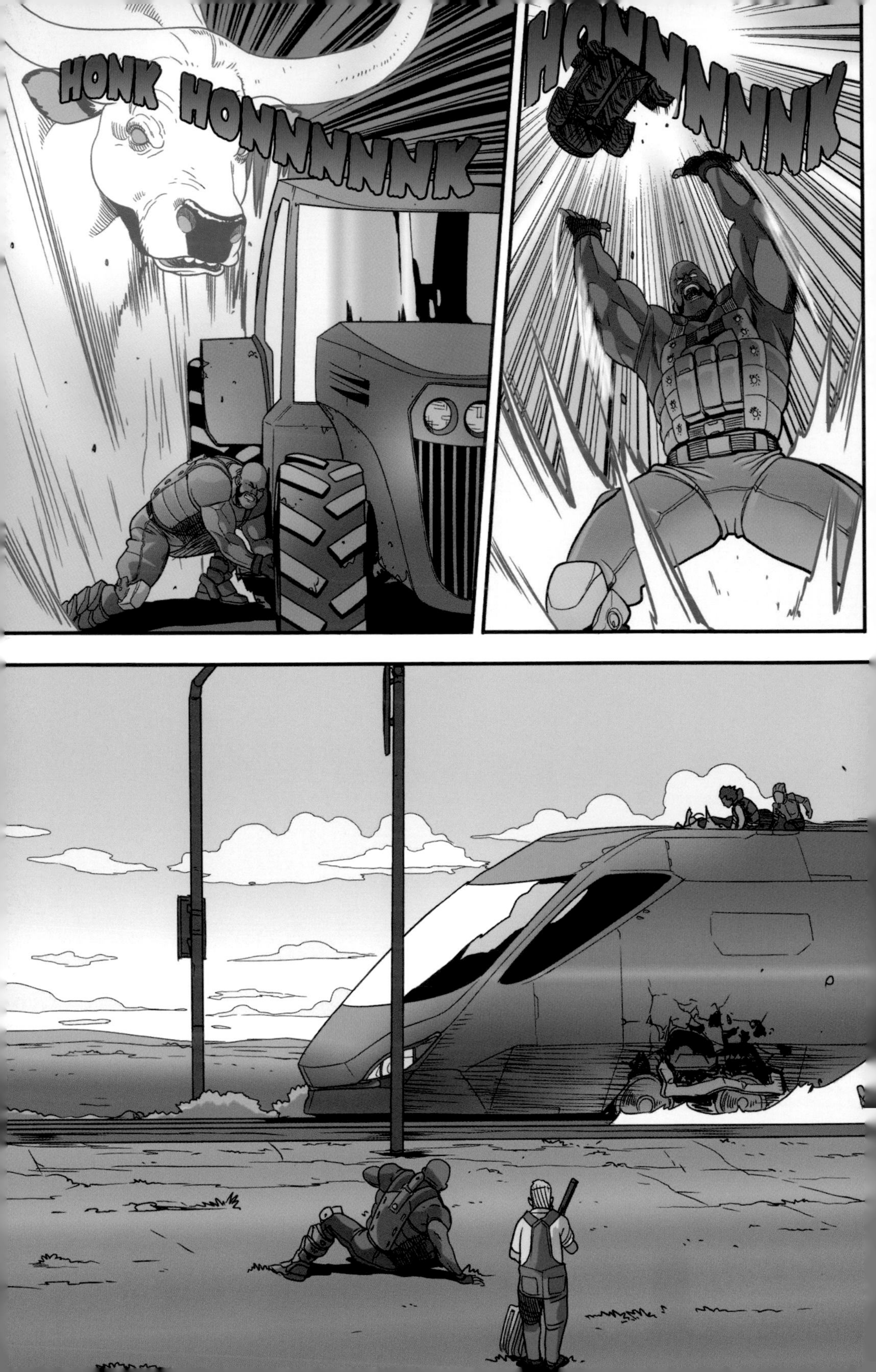
HONK HONNNNNNK
HONNNNNNNK

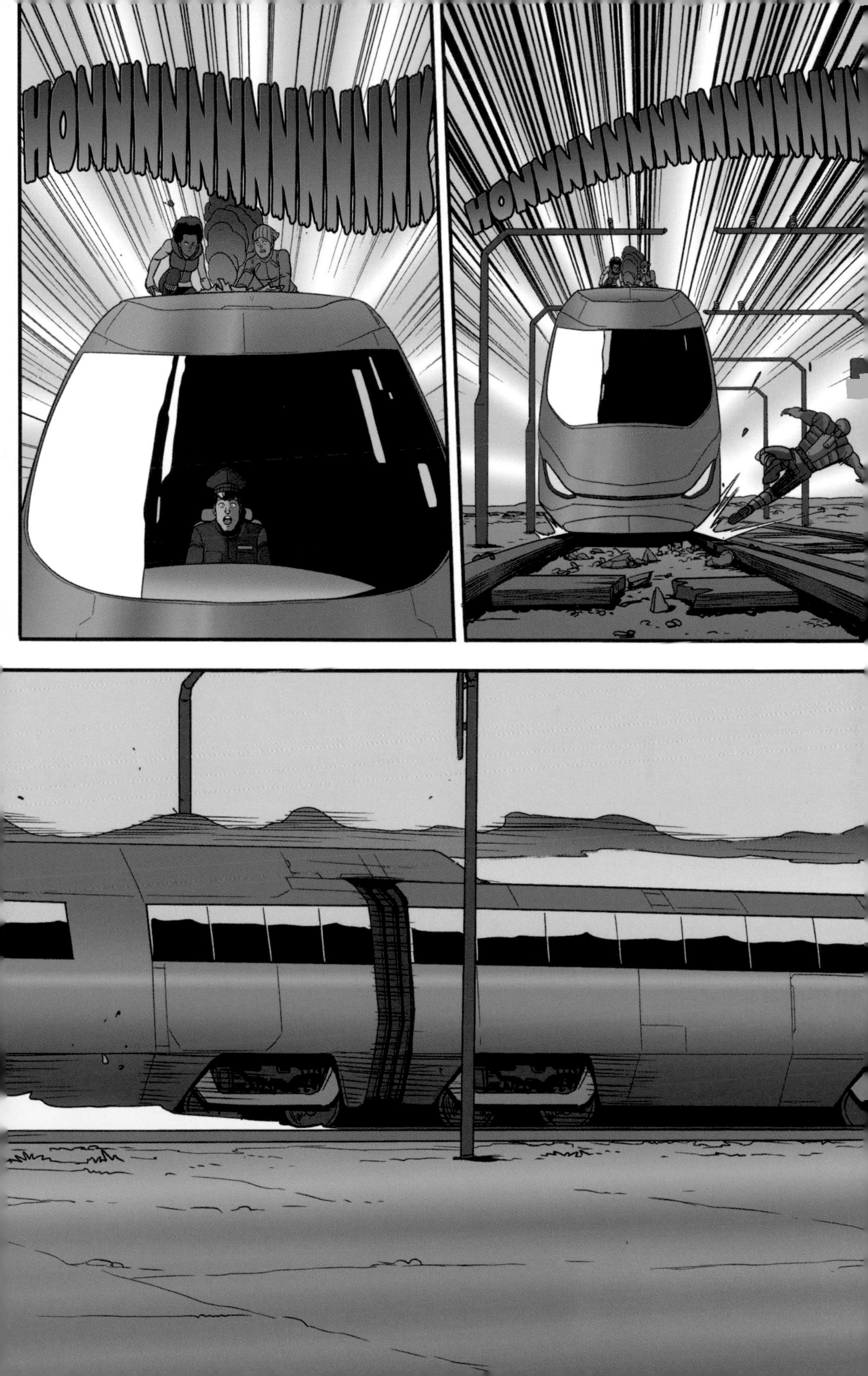
HONNNNNNNNNNNNNNK
HONNNNNNNNNNNNNNNNNNK

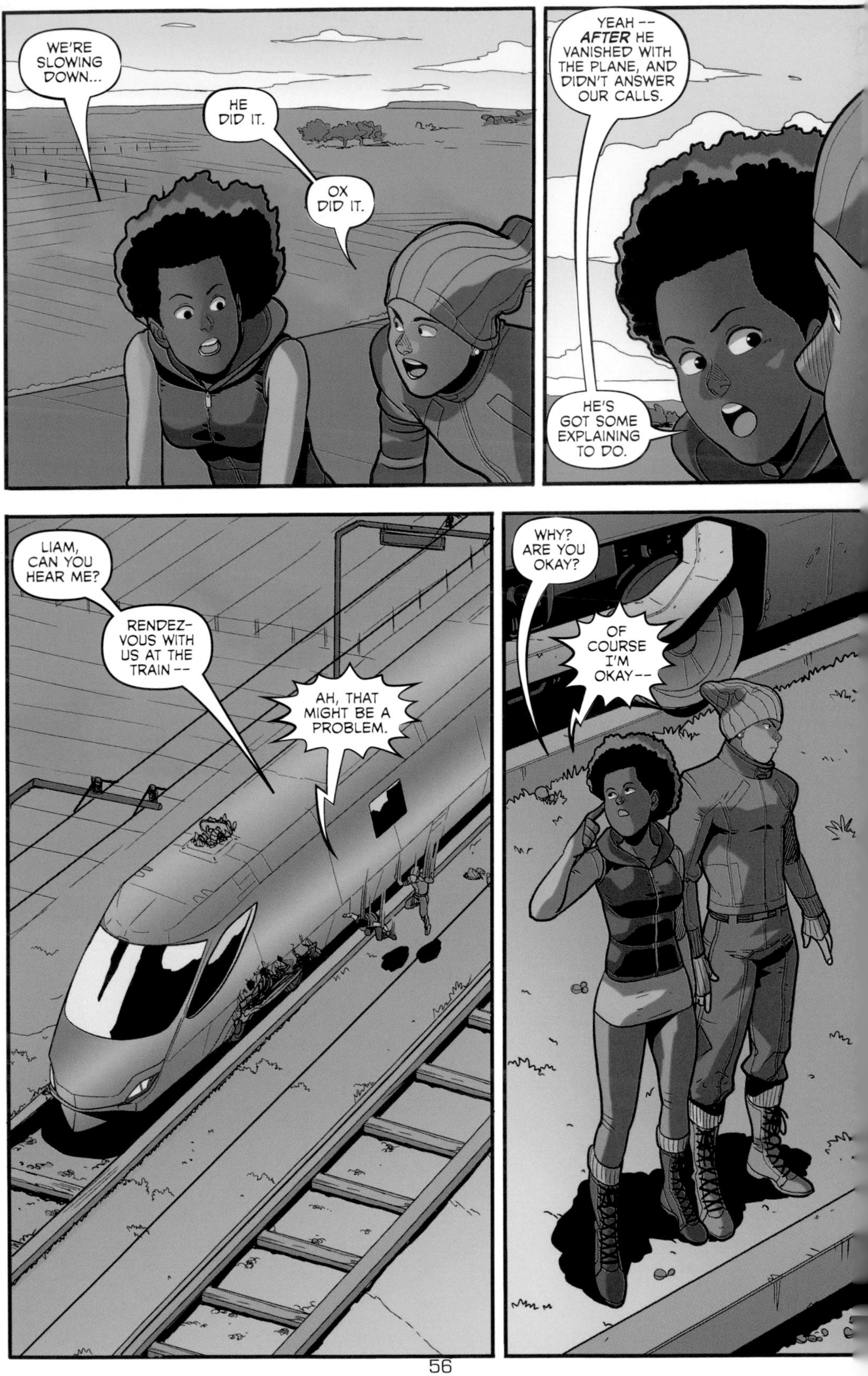
WE'RE SLOWING DOWN...
HE DID IT.
OX DID IT.
YEAH -- *AFTER* HE VANISHED WITH THE PLANE, AND DIDN'T ANSWER OUR CALLS.
HE'S GOT SOME EXPLAINING TO DO.
LIAM, CAN YOU HEAR ME?
RENDEZ-VOUS WITH US AT THE TRAIN --
AH, THAT MIGHT BE A PROBLEM.
WHY? ARE YOU OKAY?
OF COURSE I'M OKAY --

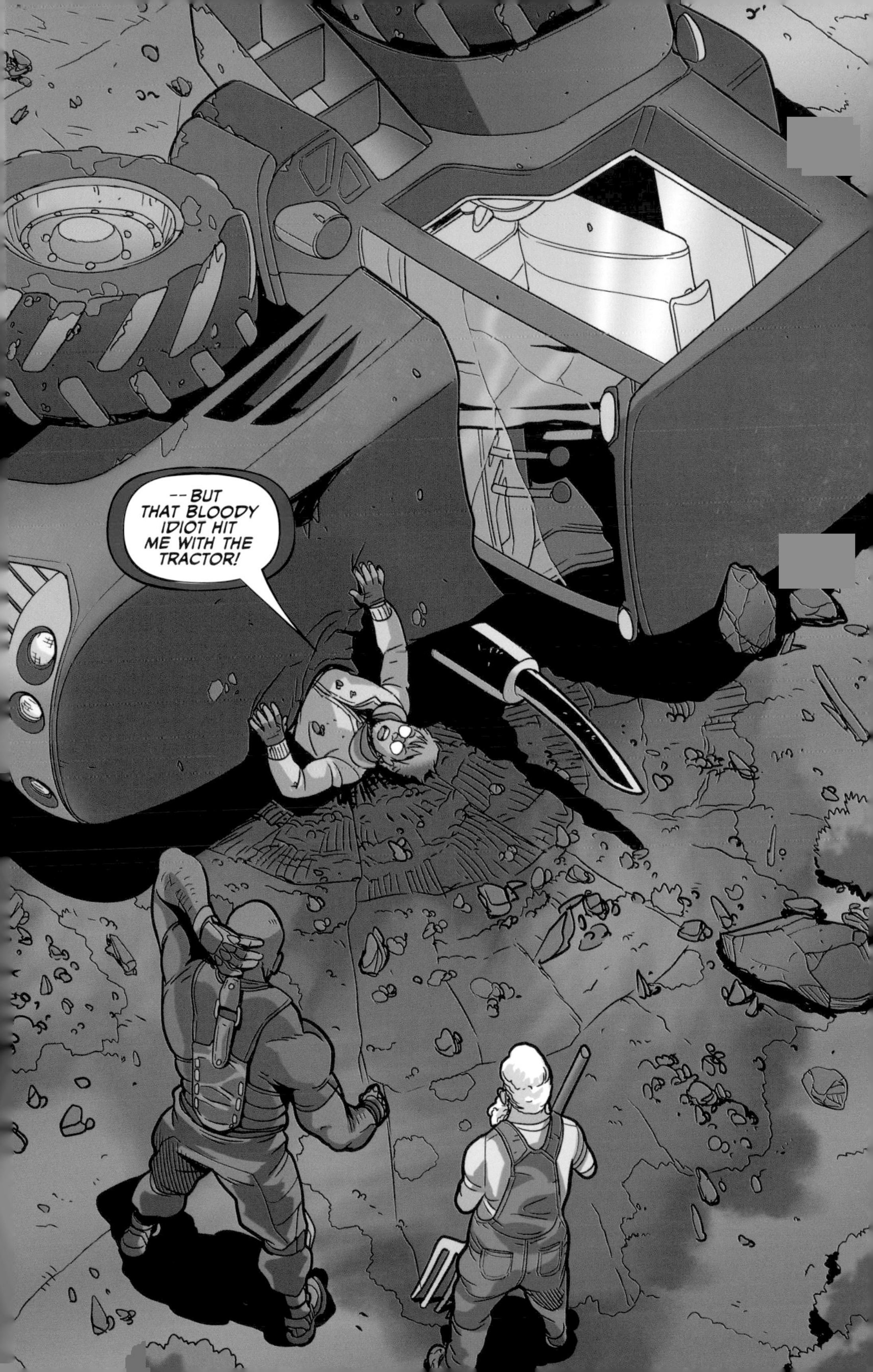
-- BUT THAT BLOODY IDIOT HIT ME WITH THE TRACTOR!

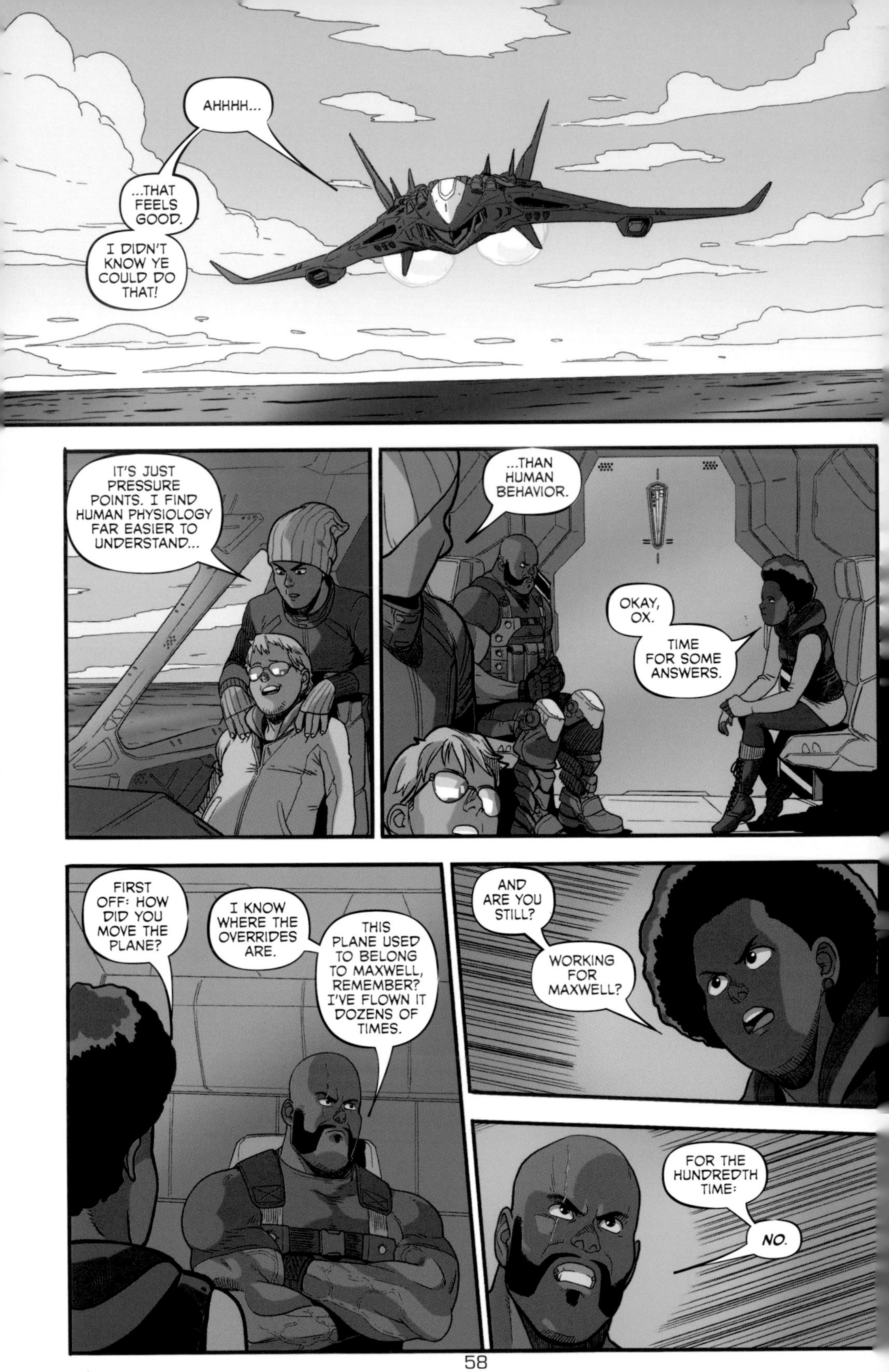
AHHHH...
...THAT FEELS GOOD.
I DIDN'T KNOW YE COULD DO THAT!
IT'S JUST PRESSURE POINTS. I FIND HUMAN PHYSIOLOGY FAR EASIER TO UNDERSTAND...
...THAN HUMAN BEHAVIOR.
OKAY, OX.
TIME FOR SOME ANSWERS.
FIRST OFF: HOW DID YOU MOVE THE PLANE?
I KNOW WHERE THE OVERRIDES ARE.
THIS PLANE USED TO BELONG TO MAXWELL, REMEMBER? I'VE FLOWN IT DOZENS OF TIMES.
AND ARE YOU STILL?
WORKING FOR MAXWELL?
FOR THE HUNDREDTH TIME:
NO.

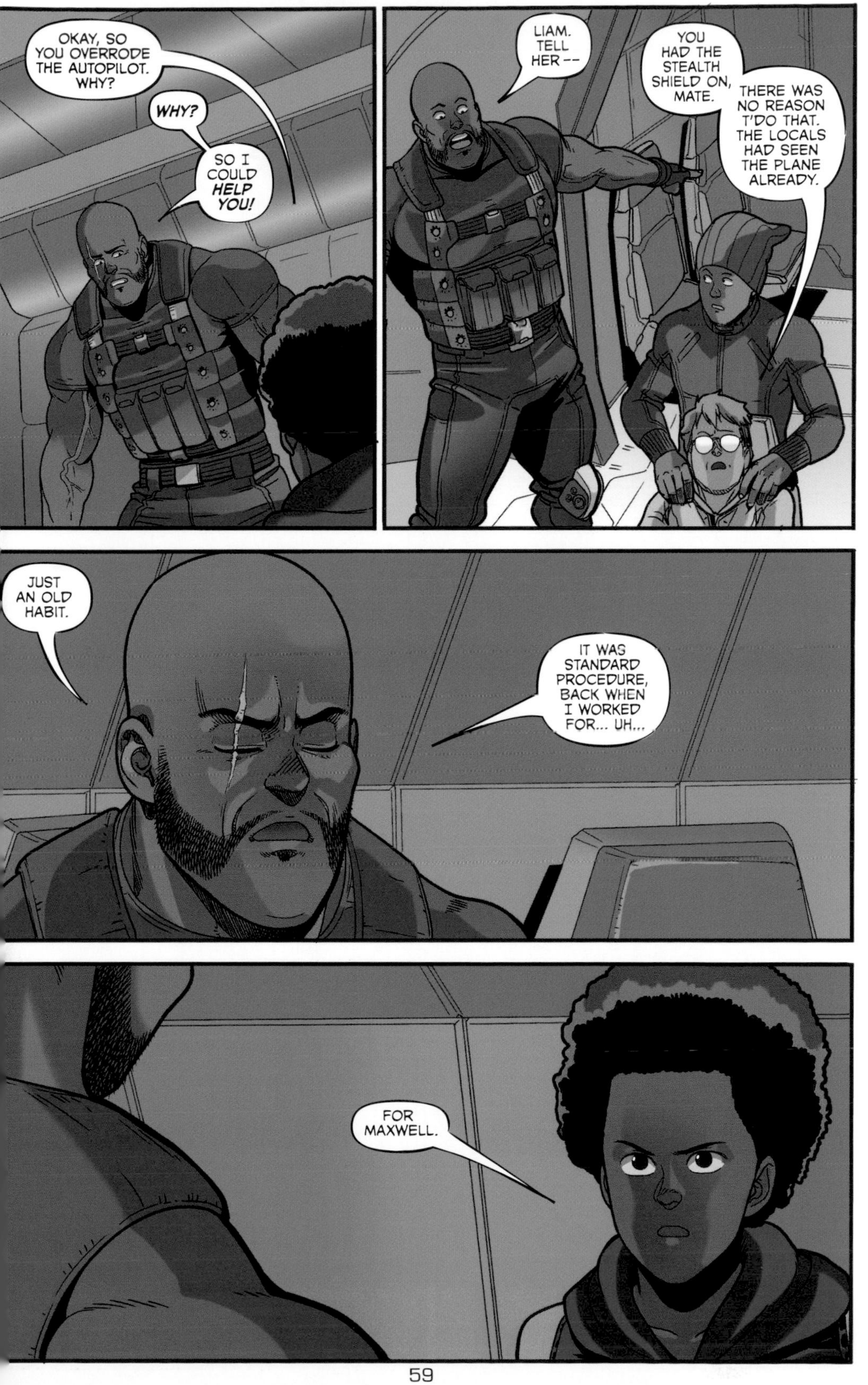
OKAY, SO YOU OVERRODE THE AUTOPILOT. WHY?
WHY?
SO I COULD HELP YOU!
LIAM. TELL HER --
YOU HAD THE STEALTH SHIELD ON, MATE.
THERE WAS NO REASON T'DO THAT. THE LOCALS HAD SEEN THE PLANE ALREADY.
JUST AN OLD HABIT.
IT WAS STANDARD PROCEDURE, BACK WHEN I WORKED FOR... UH...
FOR MAXWELL.

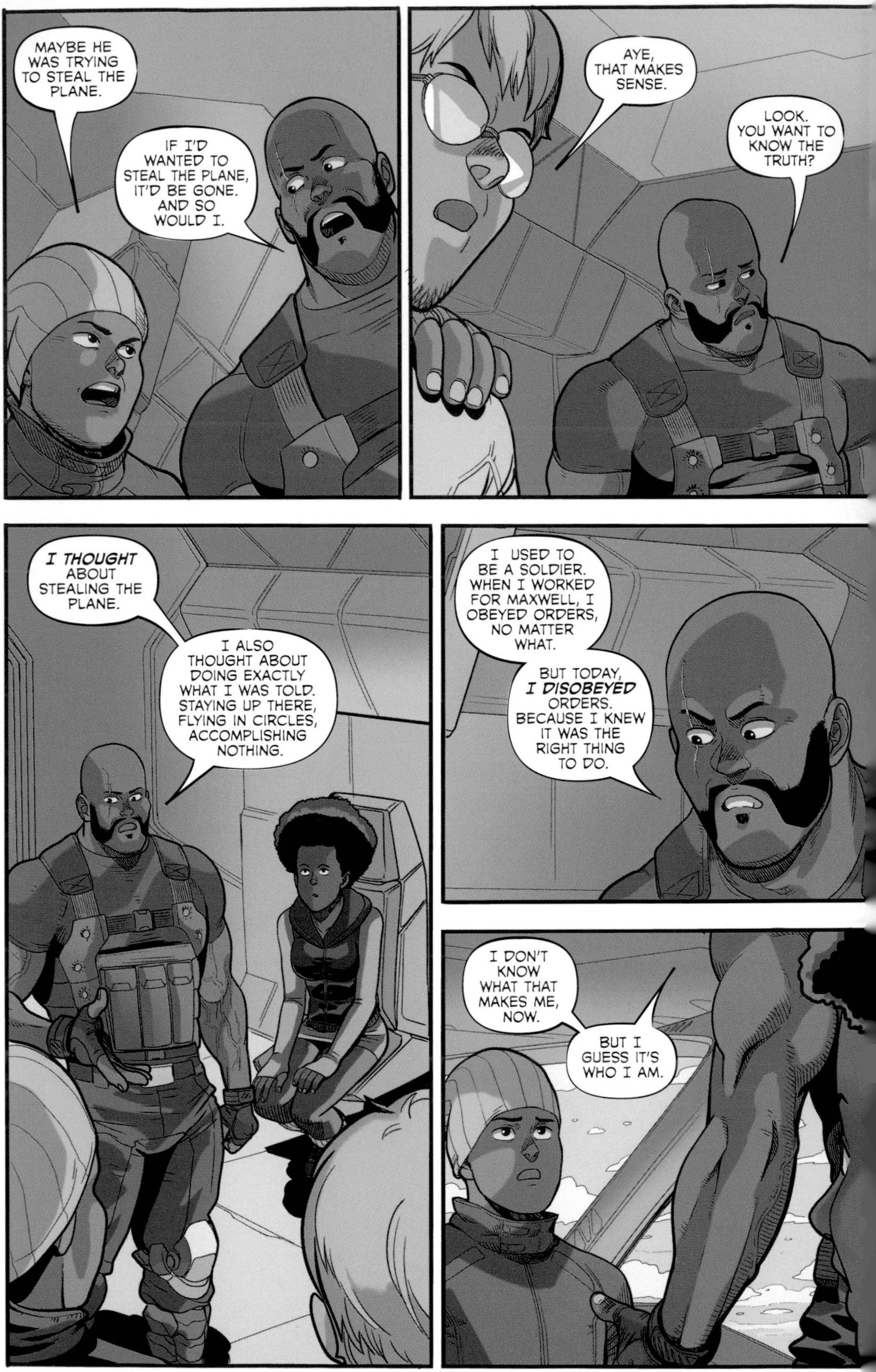
MAYBE HE WAS TRYING TO STEAL THE PLANE.
IF I'D WANTED TO STEAL THE PLANE, IT'D BE GONE. AND SO WOULD I.
AYE, THAT MAKES SENSE.
LOOK. YOU WANT TO KNOW THE TRUTH?
I THOUGHT ABOUT STEALING THE PLANE.
I ALSO THOUGHT ABOUT DOING EXACTLY WHAT I WAS TOLD. STAYING UP THERE, FLYING IN CIRCLES, ACCOMPLISHING NOTHING.
I USED TO BE A SOLDIER. WHEN I WORKED FOR MAXWELL, I OBEYED ORDERS, NO MATTER WHAT.
BUT TODAY, *I DISOBEYED* ORDERS. BECAUSE I KNEW IT WAS THE RIGHT THING TO DO.
I DON'T KNOW WHAT THAT MAKES ME, NOW.
BUT I GUESS IT'S WHO I AM.

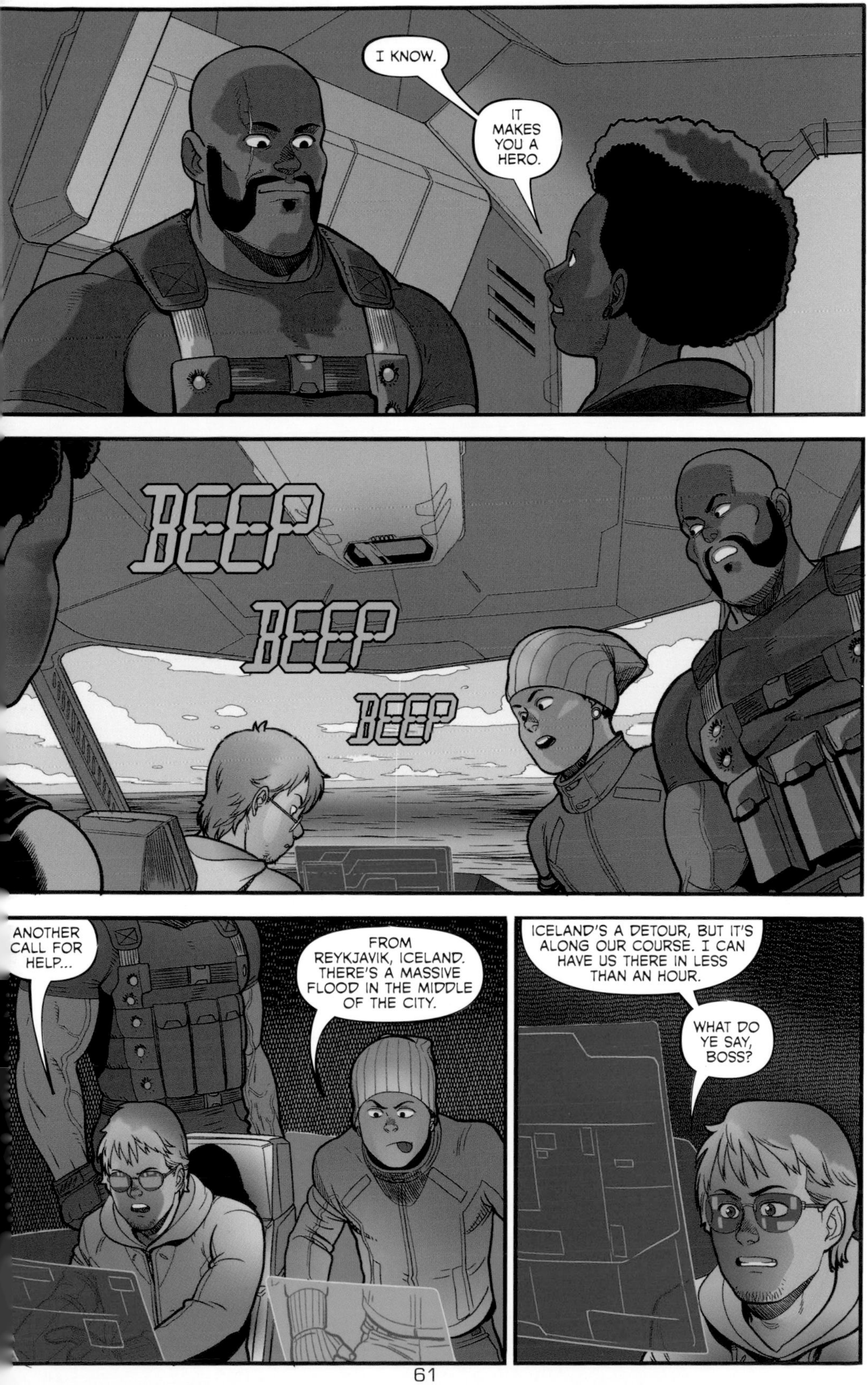
I KNOW.
IT MAKES YOU A HERO.
BEEP
BEEP
BEEP
ANOTHER CALL FOR HELP...
FROM REYKJAVIK, ICELAND. THERE'S A MASSIVE FLOOD IN THE MIDDLE OF THE CITY.
ICELAND'S A DETOUR, BUT IT'S ALONG OUR COURSE. I CAN HAVE US THERE IN LESS THAN AN HOUR.
WHAT DO YE SAY, BOSS?

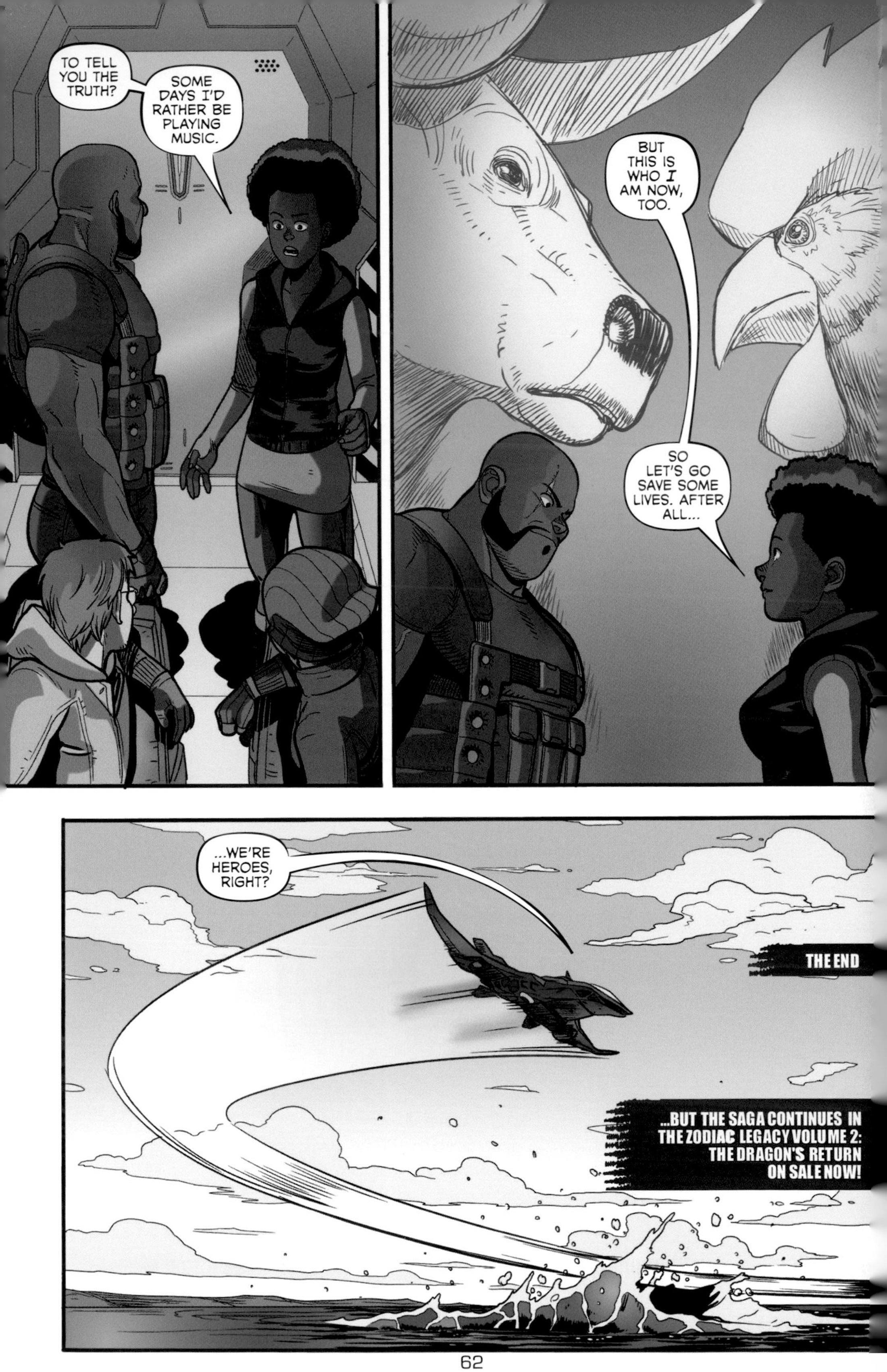
TO TELL YOU THE TRUTH?
SOME DAYS I'D RATHER BE PLAYING MUSIC.
BUT THIS IS WHO *I* AM NOW, TOO.
SO LET'S GO SAVE SOME LIVES. AFTER ALL...
...WE'RE HEROES, RIGHT?
THE END
...BUT THE SAGA CONTINUES IN THE ZODIAC LEGACY VOLUME 2: THE DRAGON'S RETURN ON SALE NOW!

WATCH OUT FOR PAPERCUTZ

elcome to the super-speedy second THE ZODIAC
GACY graphic novel series, created by Stan Lee,
ritten by Stuart Moore, and illustrated by P.H.
arcondes, from Papercutz—those subway-riding,
ily-commuters dedicated to publishing great
aphic novels for all ages. I'm Jim Salicrup,
itor-in-Chief and brother of Bill Salicrup, a
ngtime MTA (Metropolitan Transit Authority) worker.
want to talk a little bit about trains, but if I may
rail my train of thought a little, there's something
e I should mention first...

E ZODIAC LEGACY began as a series of novels
blished by Disney, written by Stan Lee and Stuart
ore, and profusely illustrated by Andie Tong. And I
n't mean graphic novels, although there are plenty
great illustrations in each book by the awesome
die Tong. I mean prose novels, in which the story
told primarily through words written by smiling
n Lee and studious Stuart Moore. Now, Papercutz
at's us!) has been working with the wonderful
ks at Disney for years, publishing DISNEY FAIRIES
turing Tinker Bell, and when we decided to add
litional Disney titles to our ever-expanding
percutz line-up of graphic novels, we couldn't
ist asking if we could create a graphic novel
ies based on the best-selling THE ZODIAC LEGACY.

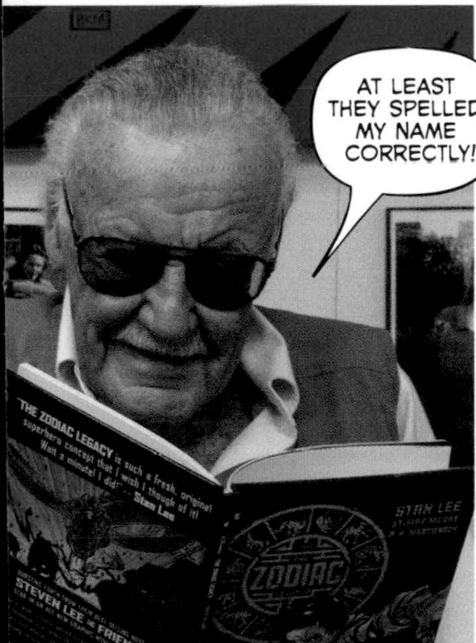
AT LEAST THEY SPELLED MY NAME CORRECTLY!
STAN LEE
ZODIAC
TIGER ISLAND

ust look at Stan Lee's face and you can tell he's inking, "Those guys and gals at Papercutz sure know what they're doing—this graphic novel is REAT!" Or at least that's what it looks like to us.

Well, obviously the answer was yes, and we really lucked out in getting the self-same Stuart Moore to agree to write the graphic novels! What sly Stuart has cleverly done is to have the Papercutz graphic novels fit seamlessly into the continuity of the prose novels. So, THE ZODIAC LEGACY graphic novel #1 "Tiger Island" fits between the first and second prose novel, and the graphic novel, "Power Line," fits snuggly between two chapters in the second prose novel (we'll let you have fun figuring out exactly which two chapters). And for those of you who may not have picked up the prose novels yet, here's what you've been missing...

On sale from Disney Press:
The bestselling THE ZODIAC LEGACY novels!

Written by **Stan Lee & Stuart Moore**
Art by **Andie Tong**

COMING SOON

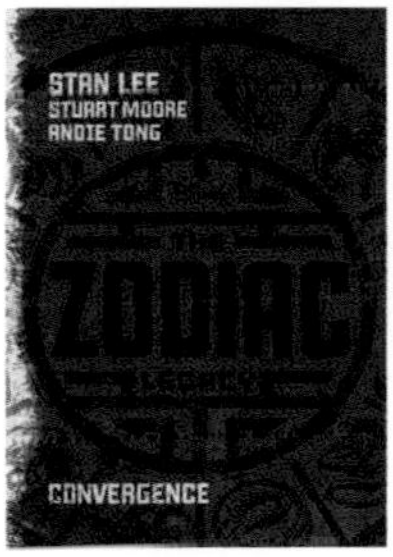
STAN LEE
STUART MOORE
ANDIE TONG
CONVERGENCE

Volume 1
CONVERGENCE
Steven Lee discovers the power of the Zodiac, and becomes part of a fantastic new team!

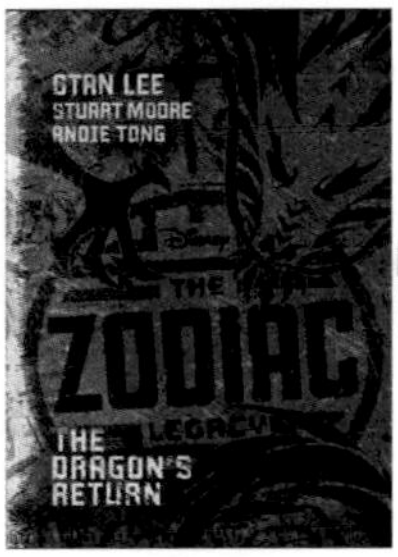
STAN LEE
STUART MOORE
ANDIE TONG
ZODIAC
THE DRAGON'S RETURN

Volume 2
THE DRAGON'S RETURN
With Steven's team falling apart, the evil Maxwell launches his ultimate plan to steal the Zodiac powers!

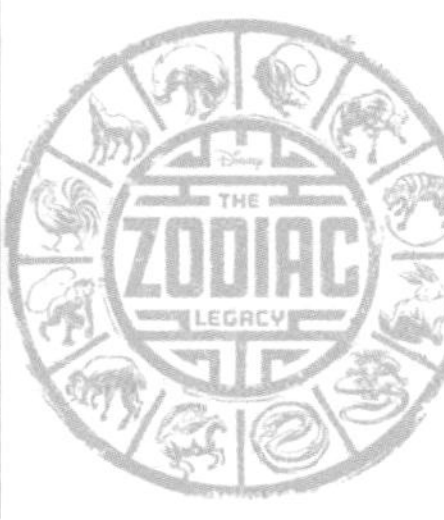
THE
ZODIAC
LEGACY

Volume 3
BALANCE OF POWER
Stripped of their powers, Steven and the Zodiacs must prevent the Dragon from destroying the world!

Gee, there's not much room left to talk about trains, is there? Well, I just have to squeeze this in: When artist P. H. Marcondes first started working for Papercutz, he drew THE HARDY BOYS graphic novels for years, and the very first HARDY BOYS graphic novel he contributed to featured a mystery that involved a runaway train! The story was called "The Opposite Numbers...," wherein Frank and Joe Hardy meet the deadly Noir Sisters. And that story, as luck and fate would have it, is included in THE HARDY BOYS ADVENTURES #1, a collected edition featuring four fantastic cases starring the teen sleuths, that's on sale now! (Guess that story was good *train*ing for THE ZODIAC LEGACY, eh?)

We hope you enjoyed "Power Lines" and you'll be back for THE ZODIAC LEGACY #3 "The Age of Bronze"!

Thanks, Jim

STAY IN TOUCH!

EMAIL:	salicrup@papercutz.com
WEB:	papercutz.com
TWITTER:	@papercutzgn
FACEBOOK:	PAPERCUTZGRAPHICNOVELS
FANMAIL:	Papercutz, 160 Broadway, Suite 700, East Wing, New York, NY 10038

STAN LEE
Creator

As if co-creating the Marvel Universe with such characters as Spider-Man, The Avengers, The X-Me Daredevil, The Incredible Hulk, Dr. Strange, and countless others, wasn't enough, Stan created a ne generation of heroes with THE ZODIAC LEGACY!

STUART MOORE
Writer
Co-Author of THE ZODIAC LEGACY prose novels, Stuart is a writer and an award-winning comics editor.

P.H. MARCONDES
Artist
P.H. has been with Papercutz almost since the beginning illustrating such best-selling titles as THE HARDY BOYS, LEGO® NINJAGO, and SABAN'S THE POWER RANGERS.

ANDIE TONG
Cover Artist
Illustrator of THE ZODIAC LEGACY prose novel, he's a comic artist, multi-media designer, and book illustrator.

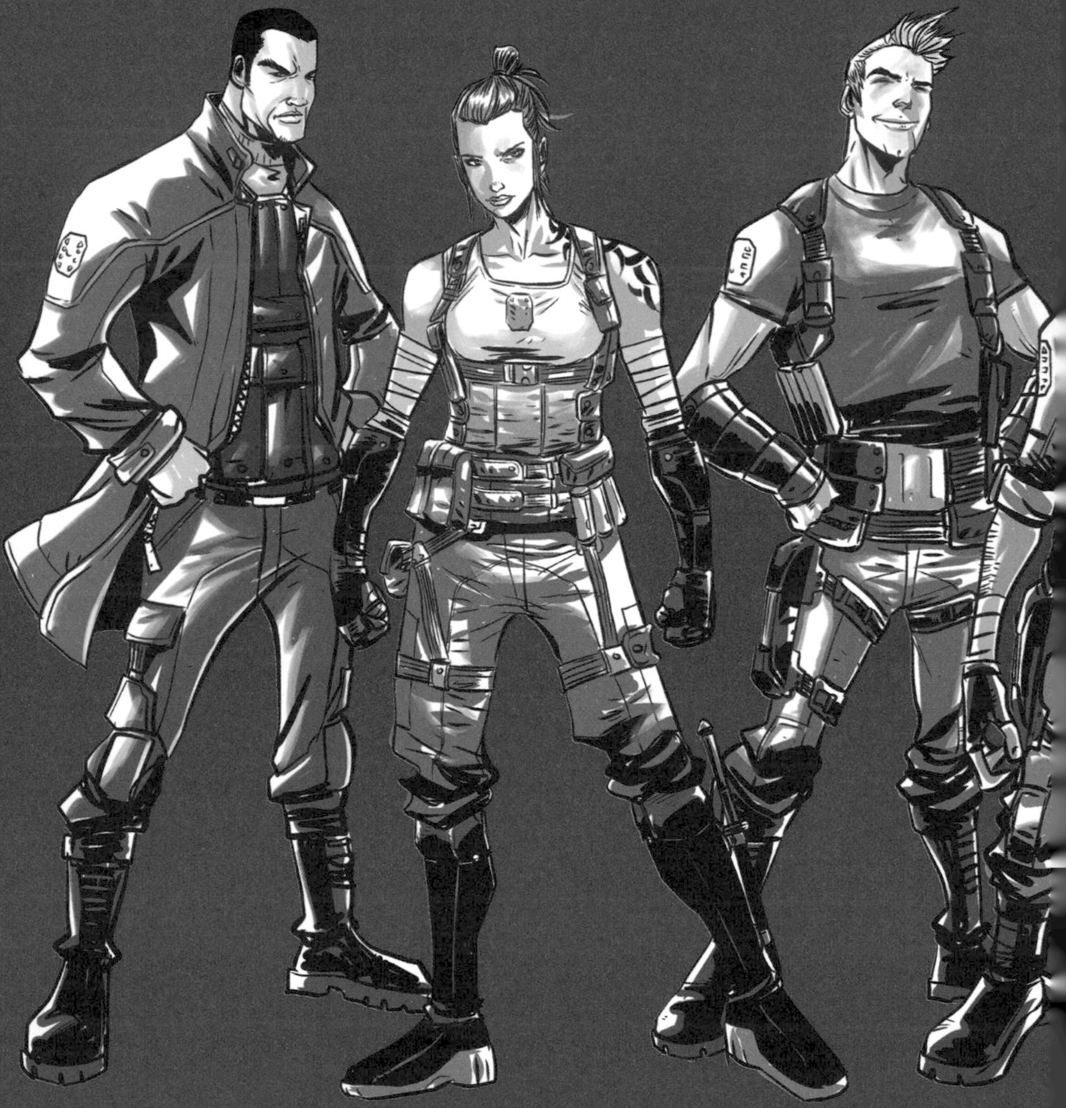